Curvy Girls

EROTICA FOR WOMEN

edited by
RACHEL KRAMER BUSSEL
foreword by APRIL FLORES

SEAL PRESS

Curvy Girls
Erotica for Women

Published by
Seal Press
A Member of the Perseus Books Group
1700 Fourth Street
Berkeley, California 94710

Library of Congress Cataloging-in-Publication Data

Curvy girls : erotica for women / Rachel Kramer Bussel, ed.
   p. cm.
  Summary: "From the editor of *Dirty Girls* comes a new anthology of steamy stories for women who don't fit into a size zero—or two, or four—and the men and women who love them. In this voluptuously erotic collection, editor and best-selling author Rachel Kramer Bussel showcases the sensual side of having "more to love," from the sexiness of big butts and plus-size corsets to the irresistible allure of pregnant bellies. No aspect of full-figured female sexuality is left unexplored, whether heterosexual or same-sex, raunchy or romantic, femme or butch. Bussel also includes seductive stories featuring characters of varying ethnic and racial backgrounds, exploring how different cultures approach size and eroticism. From trysts between long-time partners to one-night stands, from vanilla encounters to kinky romps, *Curvy Girls* is an all-inclusive celebration of the sensuality of larger women—in all their curvy glory. "-- Provided by publisher.
  ISBN 978-1-58005-408-9 (pbk.)
  1. Erotic stories, American. 2. Women--Sexual behavior--Fiction. 3. Overweight women--Fiction. I. Bussel, Rachel Kramer.
  PS648.E7C876 2012
  813'.01083538--dc23

                    2011042054

Contents

Foreword: The Voluptuous Life

For the longest time, we have been told the lie that being thin equals being beautiful, happy, and desirable. And somewhere along the line, we have also been led to believe that fat people don't enjoy sex, or possibly that we are not worthy of enjoying sex.

The main purpose of my career and work as a model and adult performer has been to show the world that these fallacies, which have been hardwired into our way of thinking, are completely untrue. I have used my body and sexuality as tools to make a statement to the world that larger women are sexual creatures who can—and do—enjoy sex, and that they should explore and express their sexuality.

Another goal of my work has been to show other bigger women that we are valuable the way we are, in the skin that we currently occupy. It seems that women are constantly made to feel that we are not valuable unless we are thinner. Daily images and messages from the media, society, family, advertising, etc., are relentlessly sent our way, and it can be very tricky to avoid feeling "not good enough." As a fat woman who has been bigger my whole life, I know how hard it can be, but I also know these notions are untrue. True happiness comes from within, and not in the form of a smaller dress size or smaller number on the scale. There are people of all sizes who are happy, and there are people of all sizes who are unhappy.

I feel very fortunate to have been given the opportunity to deliver my message, and I am grateful that my ideas have been able to reach the women I want them to reach. Nothing makes me feel more delighted than reading an email from a woman who says that seeing my work has helped her realize that she can be just as sexy as a woman half her size, or that she has started to feel more comfortable within her body while being intimate with a partner. I have cried tears of gratitude more than a few times, and reading these messages has often given me strength when the road has been bumpy.

Women enjoy sex. Fat women enjoy sex. I am one of those women and have had the extreme privilege of being able to explore and express my own sexuality within my work. I have been able to live out many fantasies while making an effort to send my message of body and size positivity. I am an exhibitionist by nature, and performing in adult films and posing for photographers and artists have allowed me to expand on my exhibitionism. I have been so lucky to have been able to broaden my sexuality by working with a diverse range of performers who represented a variety of races, gender identities, and levels of experience. With each shoot, I have learned from my partner and have been able to take away something new.

I think curvier women have become more visible than before, and that we now have stronger voices—ones that are being heard. As time has gone by, I've noticed women with a wide variety of body types, ethnicities, sexual identities, and personal styles being more expressive and completely in control of their sexuality. This change has not just been in porn, but in all forms of culture. I feel that now, more women are owning their curves and making sure their voices and opinions are heard when they feel disrespected or misrepresented.

This book is so great, because it very beautifully tells stories that cover a full spectrum of curvy women, and that show who we are in our sexuality. We are athletic, submissive, stylish, confident, and at times self-conscious. We are exhibitionists and sex workers—and so much more. We are worthy of worship. We take pleasure in our curves. We wear fine lingerie. And ultimately, we are in control.

In my opinion, confidence is what makes someone attractive. You have good sex when you feel good about yourself, regardless of your body size. The characters in *Curvy Girls* are enjoying every bit of their sexuality, and I enjoyed experiencing their sexuality, too.

— April Flores

Introduction: Curves and Attitude

When I issued the call for submissions for *Curvy Girls*, I expected to see lots of stories about women like April Flores: bold, brash, out there; women who were proud to take up space, who were proud to lust and be lusted after, who took no prisoners, in or out of the bedroom.

I did get plenty of those, but what I also received en masse were stories where positive body image played a role. That state of mind was usually something the characters aspired to (and, with the help of a lover, often acquired) more than something they started out with.

I shouldn't have been surprised. Part of my inspiration for *Curvy Girls* was my own experience as a woman with some curves I like, and others I like a little bit less. Some days I am eager to flaunt them all, and other days, I'm all about Spanx and hiding my curves.

To expect us to ignore a culture that tells us that thin-thinner-thinnest is desirable is unrealistic. So what you'll see reflected here is precisely that process of coming to terms with our curves, of standing naked in front of a mirror or a window or another person and stripping ourselves of all the preconceived notions we may have of what sexy is.

In a column I wrote about body image and sexuality, I mentioned tying up a lover and blindfolding him, and I confessed, "I got to be in control, not only in the BDSM sense, but in control of my body. I didn't feel as vulnerable as I often do when I'm naked with a lover." That is the spirit I was looking for in this book, but the flipside is also present: Many of the characters here (like many real-life women, and probably like many of you) have struggled with their bodies in various ways that have affected their sexuality —sometimes for better, sometimes for worse. Ultimately, *Curvy Girls* is a celebratory book, and one that I hope will both arouse and educate. It's about discovering what it is we want in the bedroom (and other locations) just as much as it's about claiming those desires.

In many of the stories you're about to read, women come to a place where they can be that bold, brash vixen who struts her stuff only after grappling with the underbelly, if you will, of being curvy. Take, for example, Terese, who strips in front of her window for a voyeuristic neighbor in Arlette Brand's "See and Be Seen." Another example is Maya, in Nina Reyes's "Excuses." At first Maya feels uncertain—not just about posing sexily for a sexy photographer, but also about how she will be perceived by him. Yet once she gets into her groove, she finds distinct power—and arousal—in taking it all off: "I decide to up the stakes. I stand and undo my jeans. Despite my impatience, I pull them down slowly, like I'm unwrapping a gift for him." Her body is a gift—for her as well as for him.

Aside from body image and exhibitionism, another category of stories I received focused on corsets. And why wouldn't they? These daring instruments, once worn out of social necessity, have made a voluntary comeback as women realize the instant curves a corset can provide. The man who seduces a barmaid dressed in the clothing of yore in "Wenching," by Justine Elyot, spells out for our disbelieving narrator exactly what he likes about her looks: "Think of all the words associated with a bit of extra flesh. Generous. Ample. Voluptuous. Bountiful. Beautiful, sensual words. Contrast them with their opposites: Mean. Insufficient. Meager. Miserly."

Other authors took the word "curvy" and played with it. Instead of Kim Kardashian's ass or plus-size model Crystal Renn's curvaceousness, they channeled athletes and butches. These stories made me realize that while "curvy" is often a euphemism for "fat" (a word that's being reclaimed across the blogosphere and in real life), it can also be a way to describe women who don't fit the hourglass-figure mold, and who embrace their shapes in different ways.

As I write this, activist and plus-size provocateur Nancy Upton recently brought attention to the question of just what is sexy when she won, by popular vote, American Apparel's Next Big Thing modeling contest with a series of photos in which she posed erotically with a cherry pie in between her legs, for example, and while feasting on a whole chicken. The reaction to Upton's win—and the outcry when American Apparel took away her title because she was obviously spoofing their concept of hotness—

shows that we don't just need more plus-size models. We need more plus-size role models. I hope you'll find in these pages some fictional ones who inspire you to become one.

The women in *Curvy Girls* do live up to the title's promise, yet they are much more than just their curves. They are brave, nervous, curious, pregnant, hungry, kinky, sexy. They get tattoos, spankings, dessert, and satisfaction. They aren't easily pinned down or grouped together, just as real-life women of a certain size don't think or act alike.

I hope you enjoy their adventures—and the spirit of playfulness, risk-taking, and lust that fuels them.

— Rachel Kramer Bussel

Runner's Calves

BY SOMMER MARSDEN

"How are those working out for you?"

I looked up into his face, skin the color of a decadent espresso dark chocolate bar.

"Too tight," I admitted, handing him the box of stunning black leather boots that were not in my future. "I have runner's calves."

"Sit tight. I have just the thing for you then." He moved like an athlete, smooth and sure of himself. He was tall and lean and looked like a runner himself.

I didn't get long, stringy runner muscles when I got addicted to running. I got hard, chiseled muscles that showed through leggings—and, if they were tight enough, even jeans. This was fabulous for my health and self-esteem, but not so good for my dwindling boot possibilities.

"Let's try these." He sat on that weird slanted stool they supply for shoe-store employees and pulled out all the crap manufacturers insist on stuffing inside boots. The zipper sounded almost sensual, and I was surprised when a shiver of what felt like arousal shot through me.

I put my foot in as he guided. "It's never going to happen," I tried to say, but somehow, seeing his dark hand on the pale skin of my calf, I lost my voice, and it came out in a whisper.

"I bet it will. These are vented, and they happen to be damn near magical for women who—" he paused as the zipper came all the way up "—have the same problem as you." I was in the damn boots. It was nearly a miracle.

"Chubby calves?"

"Muscular calves."

He repeated the ritual with the other boot, and before I knew it, I stood looking at myself in the mirror. Toned legs in nude stockings, a short black skirt, and boots that made me want to kick ass and take names.

"I'll take them." I searched his taut chest in its uniform-white button-down. "Chuck." The nametag was small, subtle, and gold-toned.

He gave a nod, and his grin touched something deep inside of me that inspired a sudden rush of lust. My cheeks went hot, and I shook my head. I was going gaga over a man just because he got my legs in some fine, fine boots.

"Follow me. I'll ring you up. And you should wear them out," he said. And for whatever reason, I decided to obey.

On the way to the register, I studied my calves surreptitiously in the short mirrors they peppered throughout the store.

My calves looked magnificent, my knees toned, my legs spectacular. One hundred and seventy-one dollars and change. They were worth every penny. I handed Chuck my credit card.

He eyed the card, then looked up at me. "You should let me take you out in those, Sara," he said, cocking an eyebrow and then looking away.

I laughed. Chuck was cute, but he was thin and whiplike, and I feared I would break him should we do the deed . . . which we would. "Thanks, Chuck, but I—"

"Don't like my hair?" he said, grinning. His dark curly hair was cut close to his scalp, and the suggestion made me laugh.

"No. Not that."

"Like lighter men?"

"No."

"White men?"

"No."

"Red men?" he asked, cocking his head and handing me the slip to sign.

"Um . . . no."

"Women?"

I snorted and shook my head. "A pretty girl has been known to turn my head, but no."

"Shorter, taller, smarter, uglier?" He fired them off, one by one, and slid my old boots and receipt into a bag.

"No."

"Then what?" He handed me the bag and leaned on the counter.

"Bigger," I said. I leaned in close and said, "I like my men bigger. Bigger than me. I would be afraid I'd . . . snap you, Chuck."

"Never underestimate the power of a long, lean man," Chuck said, laughing. He didn't seem offended. He didn't even seem fazed. "Where can I pick you up? Six o'clock."

I almost said no. Almost.

"I'm at 320 Willow Oak Drive. It's over by—"

"I know where it is. Six o'clock," he said and touched my hand. "Wear the boots."

Then he was gone to answer the dinging bell over the front door. The ritzy shoe store got a lot of traffic from the local business parks, and at lunchtime, it was full of women with paychecks to spend and a penchant for fine leather shoes. *And cute skinny men,* I thought, taking my bag and hustling out.

❧❧

He told me at dinner that he could keep up with me running . . . among other things. I doubted it. As lean and light as he was, I doubted he could keep up for the long haul. I managed not to maul him after dinner. I was demure and fetching in my boots as I kissed him good night, but then I tugged him by his thin red retro tie and said, "Meet me here at six. Wear your running shoes."

It was meant to echo his "wear the boots," but mine came out much more antagonistic and aggressive. His teeth flashed white in the low glow of my porch light. "Yes, ma'am." He kissed me then, and there was nothing meek about it.

I went to bed with my heart pounding as if I'd already run. I thought I'd never sleep, but I did.

He showed up bright and early wearing his running shoes,

sweatpants (thank god, call me silly, but I hate a man in running tights), and a smile. "Ready," he said.

"You'll never keep up," I declared, pulling the front door shut.

He flanked me for the first mile, lagged just a touch for the second, and pulled ahead for the third. At the end, just to show me he could, he left me in his dust. He was lounging on my front steps when I turned the corner.

"Show off," I panted.

"Sorry."

"Water?"

"Sure."

I let us in, feeling the pulse of my attraction keeping time with my pounding heart. I was wet between the legs, and it had nothing to do with running. I turned around to hand him his water, but he was right behind me, and the surprise of it made me slosh us both.

"Shit! I'm wet," I said, and then caught myself, my face blooming with even more heat—heat that had nothing to do with exertion.

"I hope so. Are you going to stop testing me now, Sara?" He dropped to his knees behind me and rubbed my calves, which were tight and flushed from running. I moaned.

"Nice," he laughed.

"Tight," I said, without thinking again.

"I bet you are," he said, chuckling. His lips found the backs of my leg, and I shivered.

I sighed and turned for him when he pulled my leggings down. His hands were amazingly dark on my rosy skin, his mouth incredibly warm. He licked the wetness from my hipbones and pressed his face to my pussy for a moment. Just an instant. I tried to pull back, realizing how sweaty I was, but then he held me fast, deceptively strong for his lean build.

"Stay still, Sara, we're both sweaty," he assured me and licked my clit until I was tugging at his shorn hair and panting like we were running again.

I came with a cry and a rush of fluid, and then strong Chuck was tugging me to the floor. "Condom?" he asked softly.

I shook my head.

"Don't be angry." He reached into the small key holder strapped to his shoe. "I was hopeful but not expectant." I laughed as the silver wrapper flashed gleefully in the sunny kitchen.

He pushed me back and lifted my legs, kissing my calves, and behind my knees, so that I jumped from the tickle. "You have the most amazing legs," he said, spreading my thighs.

"Big," I said.

"Strong."

"Manly." I had blurted out my biggest fear, and he laughed so hard it startled me.

"Hardly."

"Too big?" I tried.

"Perfect." He kissed the very fragile skin where my thighs met my groin, and I shivered. "And the skin right here is the softest thing I've ever felt." He kissed it again.

Then he was sliding into me, and we had stopped arguing about him being too lean or my thighs being too big. He moved slowly, like we had all the time in the world, and I assumed we did. My skin, still slick from the run, slid against his. Somewhere along the way, we had peeled off the rest of our clothes.

"Put your hands up," he said.

I obeyed but felt the sting of not being able to hold onto him. His lips found my shoulder even as his hands, strong like the rest of him, clamped down on my wrists and held me fast. My back pressed to the cool linoleum floor, a shard of yellow sunlight streaking over the place where our skin met. He thrust deep, and my cunt gripped around him, his cock banging and nudging all the small bundles of nerves that needed it most.

I pushed my feet down hard onto the floor, thrusting up to meet him even, as he pinned my upper body flat with his. "Nice," he said in my ear, and all the little nerves in my neck and ear danced under his breath.

"Runner's calves," I grunted, moving again, taking him deeper.

"Strong," he said.

I nodded dumbly. I was cresting that wave of an approaching orgasm, that place where my body felt desperate for release, but my mind wasn't quite ready for it all to end.

He slowed, as if reading my thoughts. No going faster here. He shifted to a nice easy rhythm that let us both catch our breath— like running, when you give yourself a moment to catch up to your racing system.

Chuck rocked his lean hips from side to side ever so slightly. I felt the bony knobs of his hipbones rub across my more padded protrusions. My pussy, slick and ready, fluttered. I gasped, biting down on his earlobe so hard he hissed.

"Cheating," he said, and pushed my wrists harder. The sharp bite of pain from those small bones grinding together had my cunt tight and my skin slippery with fresh sweat.

"Sorry."

"No, you're not," he said, bending his head enough to capture my nipple in his mouth. He moved his hands for just an instant, pinning me by the forearms now as his tongue toured the hard tip of my nipple, his teeth finding me and nipping me there hard enough to steal my breath.

I brought my legs up and wrapped them around his waist, tugging him in with my calves as I trapped him with my thighs. I clenched my pussy muscles and all of me was tight and demanding.

"Christ. Fuck." He puffed out each word as he drove into me deeper, giving up on teasing me. Giving up on a slow leisurely fuck.

"I'm going to come," I hissed. I thrust my hips up to meet him, pulled him with my legs. I fought against his strong hands, but he pinned me tight, even as I tugged him forward with my lower body.

"Shut up and kiss me," he growled.

I squeezed him once with my thighs and heard him exhale violently, and then, laughing, I kissed him, as requested. I let my legs relax, let him drive in at his own speed, let him rock those amazing hips once, twice, three times more, and then I came, whispering in his ear. I didn't even know what I was saying. Nonsense things, dirty things, filthy things, judging by the way he groaned.

He kissed me silent and went still for an instant, coming hard, yelling loud, gripping my arms with his long, cool fingers.

"Nice," I said, once we could breathe again. "And I didn't break you."

"Told you," he said, his dark eyes studying my face. The morning sun danced across his clear, smooth skin.

"You lucked out."

He shook his head, then stood up and offered me a hand. I got up, and he pressed me to the counter—both of us still nude and hot from our coupling.

"I'll admit, you're strong." He bent and sucked my nipple into his mouth. His fingers found my pussy, slipped inside to test me already.

"I am strong," I said. "I needed your special secret boots just to fit my massive calves."

"Runner's calves," he said. "Sexy, strong, kick-ass calves."

"We need a shower."

"Later."

"Don't make me trap you with my super strong thighs." I tugged him toward the bathroom upstairs, and he followed.

"Maybe in the shower," he said.

"Maybe." I took the steps ahead of him, and he stayed close behind, stroking the backs of my legs as I climbed, making the muscles dance.

"I will admit you have some strong thighs, too."

"Runner's thighs."

"Strong thighs. Sexy thighs. American thighs," he said, chuckling.

I tugged him into the bathroom and started the water.

"But you underestimated me," he said.

"I did. I admit it." I stepped in and Chuck was right behind me.

"Are you sorry?" he asked.

"I am sorry."

"Do you want to show me how sorry you are?"

We stepped under the spray, and I watched the water bead on his skin, his hair. His eyes were impossibly warm, his hands impossibly strong.

"Allow me to show my regret," I teased.

"I accept. Now, spread those thighs," he breathed, touching me.

"Runner's thighs," I said, and sighed when his fingers found me and slipped inside.

"Sara?"

"Yeah?"

"Shut up." He kissed me, his hands moving between my American thighs while I braced myself with my runner's calves.

Before the Autumn Queen

BY ANGELA CAPERTON

Betsy tugged downward at her ironed blue blouse, closing up the peekaboo gap that had arisen between the second and third buttons. It was just a temporary fix for a continual problem, but she had long abandoned embarrassment about the issue. She did everything she could to maintain a professional, neat appearance, but she accepted that little could be done with the blouse. It was part of her docent's uniform, and she had stopped fretting about it. Besides, no one had complained—at least no one had said anything to her about it—and she always wore a camisole under the blouse, so it wasn't like she was flashing skin around the museum.

She'd been working at the museum for three years—first as a volunteer, then as a paid employee. Her docent's uniform consisted of a navy-blue, knee-length skirt or slacks; the problematic light-blue blouse; and a navy-blue jacket, which bore the museum's crest above the right breast, like a little advertisement designed to draw every eye toward the ever-present pucker between her blouse buttons.

She hated the uniform—hated the way it looked, hated the way it felt. But she overcame her hatred of her mandatory outerwear with the help of private sexy underwear. She'd made her first Soma and Torrid underwear purchases impulsively, out of complete rebellion. She'd spent a lot, and as a result had to endure minimal lunches for the rest of the month. After that, she carefully planned every sexy, silky purchase so that she could fully enjoy it.

She might be the victim of the Blue Pucker of Disgrace, but she rebelled deliciously by wearing silky panties and lacy bras that hugged her curves and flattered her full figure. The creamy satin against her skin, the web of lace over her hips—they restored her identity, helped her regain her femininity. Feeling beautiful was important in a place as full of beauty as the Freiberg Museum of Art, and Betsy's intimate garments were her secret badges of identification with the painted goddesses and iconic images of classic beauty.

She'd been working at the Freiberg only six months when the head curator assigned her to the Boyton wing, her favorite. It housed the nineteenth-century European paintings and associated art—a Rosetti, a Dicksee, and a Collier, among others. But the true treasure was the large collection of paintings by the foremost American pre-Raphaelite, Corso. When Miller Boyton donated his twelve Corso oils in 1980, the Freiberg, though a small museum, became a minor shrine in the art world.

Born in Boston in 1825, August Corso was the eldest son of a successful merchant. August's father proudly sent him to study art in England, and there, the young man fell under the spell of John Ruskin. He lived for a time with the Morrises, and (according to rumor) once challenged Rossetti to a duel over a model's favors.

While other American artists were working to find an identity, Corso embraced the revival of classical romanticism and brought that passion back with him to the United States, where his paintings created an uproar for their sensuality, their depictions of full-figured partial nudes, and their rejection of the stodgy conventions of the day. He painted sixteen known works before joining the Union army and dying under a surgeon's knife after the Battle of Antietam.

Miller Boyton had gone on a personal crusade to collect Corso's paintings, and a pair of high-ceilinged halls named in his honor exhibited them, the crown jewels of the museum's holdings.

Betsy knew every brushstroke in the paintings and had almost come to think of them as living creatures, each with a personality and a story to tell. One in particular, *Autumn's Queen*, had come to hold a special meaning for her. The woman in the painting (perhaps the model Corso and Rossetti had argued over) resembled Betsy: fully fleshed, wide-hipped, and full-breasted under a veil of red, yellow, and golden leaves.

And she had a companion in her admiration. At least once a week, a young man named Fred Zims sat on the wide bench that faced *Autumn's Queen*, his lean face frozen in intent study—though in unguarded moments, when he seemed to forget he was not by himself, Betsy had seen an expression on his face that looked like lust.

Betsy had only talked to Fred a few times, but she had come to look forward to his visits. Sometimes they would be alone in the gallery—just them, the Queen, and the other five paintings—and could study the painting in quiet rapture. The lush gold and brown leaves seemed to move with the wind, and the Queen's round face—with her tranquil, half-closed eyes—almost seemed alive. The Queen stretched, ecstatic, upon an elaborate fainting couch made of vines, bent limbs, and the glowing heart of a fallen oak. She stretched, arching into the rain of leaves, her lips parted in what Betsy thought was an eternal sigh of fading bliss, her maple-red hair flowing around her face, tickling her whisper-covered breasts, blending into the autumn-littered forest floor.

Corso's works were sometimes compared to Rubens's, and though Corso's reputation was only a shadow of the old master's, Betsy understood the comparison: both had a lushness of form and color. But Corso's nymphs and goddesses were more openly sensual, even carnal. How many times had Betsy imagined herself arching against some unseen passion, kissed by the dying leaves, made love to by the mists of a tired sun? And while Betsy's hair wasn't the same fire-rich auburn as the Queen's, her reddish-blond locks sometimes flashed with the same golden highlights.

Today, for the first time ever, Betsy half-dreaded Fred's arrival, though she knew he would certainly come. He must have heard the news.

When her young man entered the hall, he stopped before the Queen, as he always did. This time, however, his face didn't shine with dreams or desire, but with a sorrow that bruised Betsy's heart. She stood at her post by the door and divided her focus between Fred and a few college students who cruised through the wing with impolite speed. Fifteen minutes later, only Fred remained. This time, he was not on his bench, but standing, like a

Buckingham Palace guard—unmoving, almost catatonic, staring at the painting as if he could devour it with his gaze.

She approached him carefully, just to his left, careful not to obscure his vision but within his line of sight.

"You know?" she asked quietly.

"Yes. Yes, I do," he whispered.

"She'll be back. It's only a year, and the Met will take good care of her."

He looked at Betsy, blinking as if trying to clear his eyes of dust . . . or fantasies. "I'm going in June."

He looked back at the painting, the intensity in his eyes hot enough to bore holes through marble. What would it feel like to be burned by such a gaze?

"You'll be here tomorrow for the opening of the Waterhouse exhibit?" she asked, just to buy a moment. She needed to be part of his worship, to understand the aura of love that flowed from him like rich cream.

"I might go to the reception tonight, but I don't know. Waterhouse is all right, but he's not Corso."

"No, he's not," Betsy agreed.

Fred didn't say anything more, and Betsy's stomach tightened with the discomfort of the silence. She turned to leave him to his communion.

"You could have been one of his, you know."

Betsy's mouth suddenly went dry. "I'm sorry?" she said, turning back to him.

His cheeks flushed with embarrassment. "I mean, you could have been one of his models. He preferred generous models."

Betsy blinked twice, then grinned. "Generous. I like that."

Fred turned to the painting. "Me, too. Look at her. Look at the light on her skin, the softness and grace of it. She is full, a complete woman. I see such truth in her curves."

"Truth?"

"You know what they say: 'Art shows us the things we desire.'" He was quoting a brochure, which featured a quote from the museum's founder, Samuel Freiberg. She finished the quote: "'Art shows us the things we can be.' Listen. Come to the reception tonight? You won't be sorry." A giddy, girlish excitement blasted through her. Her belly warmed, and between her thighs, a slow, promising wetness flowed.

"All right," he said, and she felt his gaze as she crossed the gallery to resume her vigil. She had to struggle not to giggle at the silly, romantic image in her mind: Fred challenging Rossetti to a duel.

❦

That night, in the east corner of the hall, music rose from a small quartet, its understated strings weaving illusions of mist. Betsy wore the knee-length skirt and kept her blazer buttoned up to reveal only a little of the pucker-prone blouse beneath. She mingled with the guests and enjoyed the energy of the crowd—artists, patrons, a few minor celebrities, and the guest of honor, Reginald Foster, the head curator of the Brightman, where the Waterhouses usually resided. Foster was charming everyone with humorous stories of masterpieces lost and recovered, but Betsy's attention repeatedly returned to the door.

When Fred finally arrived, only a few minutes remained before the unveiling of the first Waterhouse. Betsy politely disengaged herself from a conversation with a steel-haired woman wearing a large diamond broach whose weight seemed to pull her upper body downward into a perpetual hunch. She skirted the crowd and reached him, smiling.

"I'm glad you made it, Mr. Zims. They're about to get started."

He nodded, taking a glass of wine from a waiter's tray. "It looks like quite an event."

"We're proud to have the exhibition. It will be a nice draw while the Queen is away."

At the mention of his icon, Fred's color retreated a little, but he nodded. "Will you continue to work the Boyton wing, or will you move here?"

"No, I'll stay with the remaining Corsos. I like Waterhouse well enough, but . . ."

Fred smiled for the first time that evening. "He's no Corso."

Besty grinned. She glanced around the room, watching as the crowd slowly shuffled toward the far end of the hall, where a red velvet curtain hid a wall of treasures. She slid her hand into Fred's and felt him stiffen, then relax into formal wariness. She couldn't blame him for reacting that way. She spent her days discouraging people from touching things, yet here she was, holding his hand. She had broken a wall between them. Perhaps she had made a mistake? As though he understood her worry, his hand tightened around hers reassuringly, showing acceptance of the breach.

"Come with me," she breathed.

He looked into her face, his strong jaw clenched in a line of thought. He took another sip of the wine, set the half-full glass onto a passing waiter's tray, and then turned to Betsy and nodded. She led him by the hand, and he followed, out of the lights and music and into the shadows of the museum.

As they approached the floor-to-ceiling glass doors that sealed the Boyton wing, she slipped her hand free and opened the security panel. She punched in a code, and the green light acknowledged her clearance. She opened the glass doors just enough to admit the two of them, and she led him through the first Corso room—lit only by security lamps, dim as candlelight—and then into the chamber of the Queen.

"You planned this," Fred said, his hand warming in hers.

"Yeah, I did. I know how much she means to you."

The low, smoky light shadowed the edges of the Queen's frame, but as Betsy's eyes adjusted, the rich flesh and golden leaves—vivid in memory, but now muted into darkly romantic tones of mahogany and sienna—seemed to glow with their own illumination.

Betsy turned her back to the Queen and faced Fred. She didn't think, barely heard the distant violins, as she unbuttoned her blouse to expose ample breasts cupped in a lacy black bra— the plunge deep in restraint, the globes held in place by delicate silk and strong satin.

Fred's gaze bathed her, and a blush of warmth effervesced in her toes and rose through her body like steam. She was terrified at her own boldness, but also excited and slick with wanting this, so she forced herself to relax. She wanted to leap at him, pin him down, and show him what a true earth goddess was all about. Instead, she shrugged off her blouse, her skin blooming in the sudden adoration, her mind alive with the actuality of revelation.

"She would approve," she whispered in the golden gray light, extending her hand to him. Fred didn't blink, didn't move, a gorgon's prize as he assessed her against the exquisite background of a windy autumn night, in the court of the Autumn Queen. Suddenly, the fear of rejection needled her breasts and hollowed her belly. Her extended fingertips ached with want, pulsed with her blood's wild flow, but when he extended his arm and clasped her hand, her knees began to tremble. In that moment, she didn't care if the world disappeared.

It wasn't gentle or romantic—his pull was possessive and strong, and her pussy dripped, soaking the thin slice of material between her legs. His lips claimed hers, branded her with such lust, she didn't know if her heart could take the force. His tongue pressed hers into submission as his hands kneaded her back and waist, cupped her ass, and pulled her tight against his hips, the impressive line of his cock a rod of jumping life against her thigh.

He broke the kiss and pushed Betsy out to arm's length. He looked around the dark hall, then up at the Queen, his face a mosaic of conflict.

"She drops her leaves, golden and rich, and gives herself to an invisible lover," Betsy said. She unbuttoned and unzipped her skirt, let it drop, and stepped out of the puddle of blue. She stood straight, the sheer stockings held up by garters, the belt low on her round hips. She didn't shrink away from his appraisal, her nipples hard bumps within the cups of her bra, her belly a soft swell. He looked at the painting, then back at Betsy, and she glowed at his comparison. When his gaze held, Betsy blushed all over. He reached out and traced a finger along the outline of her bra, stoking the skin to thin lines of fire.

"I'm not invisible," Fred said, his words slow and creamy. "I'm here. I'm real."

He slid his fingers under the edge of her bra, sliding them back to the clasp, and deftly unhooked it. Betsy drew in a sharp pull of cool air as he freed her body. As the globes of her breasts fell from the cups and into his hands, a low vibration echoed in his throat, a feral sound that melted her. Her pussy ached with wanting, with the need of feeling him inside her. His fingers caressed her full, heavy breasts, teasing the nipples to even harder peaks, cradling them in his hands before he lowered his head and worshiped them. She wanted to scream, wanted the glorious sensation of his mouth lapping and suckling her breasts to be known to the world, but instead, she bit her lip and stared up at the Queen, exuberance hers as the wild excitement of being blessed by this manifest deity rained down upon her. Fred's lips and teeth exploited her breasts, his enthusiastic appreciation of their size and sensitivity beyond her imagining. As if the ravished tits were wired directly to her pussy, Betsy's clit tingled and pulsed, her wetness almost embarrassing.

She tugged at his belt, needing his stiff cock in her hands before he put it into the wetness. Lowering his trousers and pulling his cock through the slit of his boxers, she bolted closer to orgasm as her fingers closed around it. It was eight inches and generously veined; her mouth watered now, too.

He kissed her, hot and hungry, then slid his hand into her panties, fingers instantly coated in her juices.

"My god," he groaned against her mouth. He circled her clit, the flesh slick with need, and Betsy moved against his hand, following the rhythm of his possessive strokes. He kissed her neck, nipped along her shoulder, and relentlessly fingered her. As the orgasm crested, he sealed her cry with his lips, her body one blessed exposed nerve, limbs trembling and golden light crashing over every inch of skin. His kiss held her, owned her, as if he was taking her pleasure through his lips and tongue.

She panted, and her heart raced as he broke the kiss and smiled at her. He brought his fingers to her lips, smeared her juices onto them, then kissed her again. "You're delicious," he whispered, "and I want more."

He moved her to the end of the wide bench in front of the Queen and kissed her as he sat her down onto the dimpled leather. He gently pushed her back, but Betsy resisted.

"No, wait," she whispered, and stood up again, the wicked delight of her inspiration as exciting as his questioning, almost fearful look. She moved to stand with the bench between her and the painting and removed her drenched panties. When she knelt on the wide expanse of leather, her legs spread and ready for him, she looked back and saw Fred's cock visibly jump. She grinned, thrilled to see the mix of shock and lust gloss his eyes. She crooked her finger, inviting him in.

He quickly dropped his pants and his boxers, the glistening tip of his cock shining amber in the low lights of the hall. He stepped behind her, into the saddle of her stocking-covered legs. Heat radiated from him, and though her pussy still tingled from his fingers, she wanted his cock buried deep inside her—and she wanted it here, with her, the Queen of his obsession. Was she offering herself to some higher power, or to Corso's ghost? She felt divine, a priestess, a celebrant in some faith as old as mankind. She knelt, a sacrifice to art patronage, willing to give as much as she took.

As his hand stroked and kneaded the soft flesh of her ass, she arched, her breasts hanging down, her belly round and tight. He stroked her pussy again, cupping it, rubbing her clit between his index and middle finger. She moaned—so hot, so ready—staring at the Queen and basking in the benediction of color and timeless beauty, bare before her and ready for her to bless the moment.

When his cock slid along the outside of her pussy, she squirmed, wanting the hot flesh to be inside her. He didn't tease her for long. When his cockhead rested at the gate, her first instinct was to push back—to envelop him and clench tight, locking him in—but she resisted, allowing him the filling stroke. When his cock entered, she gasped, amazed at how glorious he felt, the generous girth filling her perfectly. He slid in all the way, didn't stop until his balls touched her pussy lips, and she soared high on the thick wave of pleasure each inch gave her. Then he froze, didn't move, just stayed buried in her, and she looked back over her shoulder at him. He was staring at the painting, just as she had, and a needle of jealousy pricked her heart.

Until he began to move.

His rhythm was maddened, hard, demanding. He fucked her, and she reveled in the hard slam of his cock into her, in his greedy hands gripping her belly, groping her breasts, slapping her ass. She ground back against him, equal in her passion. He reached around her, stroked her clit, rocketing her reckless beyond sweat and flesh into nothing less than nirvana. The orgasm ripped through her, exposing her spine to air, baring her heart to the shared heat and lust. Her body trembled, her vision watered, the golden Queen blurred into a window of renewal, born of precious, shared flames.

He came in her, filling her, their spend dripping onto the leather and the floor. Both of them struggled for breath, but as his cock softened, he continued to thrust into her, the wet finishing strokes precious to her, the final prayer of a powerful ritual.

She sank onto the bench, her legs spreading wider. When his cock slipped out of her, Fred wrapped his arms around her, holding her tight against him. They moved onto the bench, spooning on the cool leather, both of them facing the Autumn Queen, their breath returning to normal, their bodies sticky and whole.

Betsy stared at the painting, loving the sensation of Fred's hands lazily exploring the layers of her flesh. The Queen, frozen for eternity, arching toward an unseen hand, didn't frown, didn't smile, but remained unchanged—and yet Betsy saw her new, the red of her hair just a little more lively; the leaves, suspended in time, were filigree treasures of perfect brushwork. *This moment would never come again,* Betsy thought with a twinge of sadness. What followed such transcendence?

She stroked Fred's arm and lifted his hand to her lips, kissing it lightly. "What do you see when you look at her, at the Queen?"

He kissed the back of her head and squeezed her just below her breasts. "What do I see? Don't you know?" He nuzzled her neck.

"I see you."

Champagne & Cheesecake

BY A. M. HARTNETT

She called them her "victory tits."

A whole year without smoking, and Sylvia had packed on thirty pounds, but she was no longer sorry for a single ounce of the blubber. In fact, now that she was staring at her reflection in the full-length mirror of the luxurious hotel room, she was feeling pretty good about the added girth. Her round face was even rounder now and was perfectly framed by newly tinted red curls. Her corset was cinched to accentuate her shape without diminishing what was there. The demi-bra was snug but not too snug, lifting her tits just enough to accentuate their plumpness without overflowing.

Sylvia struck a hand-on-hip pose. She'd been tempted to go with the ruffled boyshorts, but in the end, she hadn't been able to resist the lure of the lacy red panties-and-garters combo.

Traditional and irresistible, and nicely paired with black stockings, the kind with the seam along the back.

She went to the closet and slipped on her five-inch heels, then returned to the mirror for another look. She wasn't yet used to carrying around an extra thirty pounds, and she felt it more on her feet than anywhere else, but the heels made her look and feel like a bombshell, so she sucked it up.

She lifted her hair off her neck and blew a kiss at her reflection. The image was so bombshell. She couldn't help but laugh out loud as she let her hair tumble over her shoulders, leaving her appearance softer than before.

Her boys were going to go crazy when they saw what she had to offer now.

⚜

She'd been keeping her appointment with Vaughn and MacLean for ten years now. They'd met in an Internet chat room for sci-fi geeks, way back when they were all still in college. The two boys had been part of a group plotting to meet in Chicago, where Sylvia was, for an upcoming convention, but as the months turned to weeks, everyone else in the group dropped out—either too poor or just not serious enough—and Sylvia was left with the prospect of playing host to two University of North Carolina students en route to their home bases in Minneapolis.

The first night, they'd all gotten too drunk to stand. The second night, they'd stayed up all night playing video games. On the third night, they'd cracked open a bottle of wine and started fooling around in front of the fire. The first had been Vaughn, who was sheepish when Sylvia pulled his cock out of his shorts and started sucking him. In the beginning, MacLean was content to watch, but after a while, he moved behind Sylvia and unzipped.

Since then, they'd grown up, graduated, and gotten jobs. As for Sylvia, she'd finished school in Chicago and continued to live and work there. Vaughn settled in Arizona, and MacLean bounced around for a while—from Seattle to California to as close as Indianapolis—before landing his dream job in Hawaii.

Sometimes it seemed impossible that they were all still unattached, still in touch, still meeting up every summer. Sometimes, but not today.

∽⚬∂⚬∾

Covering up her ensemble by slipping on a little black dress, Sylvia swept a quick gaze around the luxurious hotel room—a king suite with a lake view, Jacuzzi tub, a shower big enough to fit three, and champagne chilling on the table by the window. Though she still lived in Chicago and could easily have the boys at her place, there was something about fucking in a hotel, even a nice one, that made it dirtier. And the cost wasn't a problem: She'd used the money she saved by quitting the smokes to pay for the room.

She was checking out the enormous bathroom when she heard the door beep and the men enter. Excitement swirled through her belly as she stepped out of the bathroom to greet them with a big smile.

MacLean, dark and bespectacled, was in front and the first to look upon her. As his gaze went from head to toe, a sprig of self-consciousness broke through the surface of Sylvia's confidence. She crossed her arms over her chest and flushed. MacLean's green eyes softened. "I know I already told you on video chat last night," he said, "but I have to say it again. You look unbelievable."

"I know what you mean," Vaughn chimed in. "Sylvia, you look better than ever. I've been dying to get my hands on what I could only see on the screen."

Sylvia smiled. "You have to say that. Otherwise I might change my mind and leave you here to watch porn by yourselves all night."

Vaughn approached her and slipped his arms around her waist. "You're so wrong on both counts," he said. "I don't have to say a damn thing, and you're not going anywhere." As he lowered his mouth to hers, she cupped the back of his head and tightened her fingers in his reddish hair. It all felt so natural. She still felt small in his arms, and the flowing, euphoric feeling banished any thought of being too big now.

Vaughn's hands slid across her hips and over the hump of her ass. With his stiffening cock pressing between her legs, Sylvia forgot all about feeling self-conscious, or even feeling like a bombshell. She forgot about victory tits and garters and ten-year anniversaries. She even forgot that there was someone still missing from the equation—at least until a low chuckle from MacLean reminded her.

Sylvia broke away from Vaughn and giggled as she looked to MacLean. "Look at you, always waiting your turn. Come and give me a hug, like you should have done when you first walked in."

"How could I, with his hand on your ass and his tongue in your mouth?"

Vaughn snorted. "In my defense, my tongue never got a chance to get into her mouth."

MacLean's embrace was different, more exploratory. The hug was quick, and then his hands were on her shoulders, pushing her hair away from her neck. Sylvia wet her lips and held her breath as he brushed his mouth over hers. His hot tongue darted across her lower lip and back again, touching hers midway. She moaned. Heat zipped from the tip of her tongue to her toes while his hands moved down to her breasts. He brushed his thumbs over the hard peaks pressing against the taut bodice, and a heavy heat settled between her legs, spawning an ache she knew wouldn't be sated completely for hours.

The kiss ended, and he withdrew. She was woozy on her feet as they stood side by side and regarded her. There wasn't an ounce of self-consciousness left in her body. She felt desirable and electric with what was to come.

Clearing her throat, she turned and headed toward the mini-bar. "Why don't I play hostess for one of you while the other showers. Then we can order up some room service, crack a bottle, and get this party started."

Having flown nonstop for eight hours, Vaughn hit the shower first and could be heard moaning his relief as he stood under the spray. Sylvia had a Captain and Coke waiting for him when he emerged, the same drink she had prepared for MacLean.

By the time the meal arrived, both men looked fresher. When Sylvia finished her cheesecake and coffee and melted back in her chair, comfortably full, it was already growing dark outside. MacLean turned on a couple of table lamps, then watched her a moment. "Is it killing you, not smoking after dinner?"

"Oh, hell yeah. After dinner, after a cup of tea, and after an orgasm."

Vaughn leaned back and folded his hands behind his head. "So tonight you might be sent screaming back to the smokes. 'Screaming' being the key word here."

"I don't think so. I've had a lot of practice," she said. "Though maybe that's the equivalent of someone who's used to running a 5k saying they're ready for the Boston marathon." It would definitely be a new challenge.

MacLean gathered the plates onto the tray and carried it to the door. When he returned, he was grasping the champagne bottle by the neck.

"I feel like we should have something more extravagant planned," he said. "It's been ten years since we met—plus one year since Sylvia kicked the smokes."

Vaughn nodded. "He's right. We should have gone to a resort or something."

The champagne was uncorked with a pop, and Sylvia held out her glass to be filled. "Come on," she said. "You can't beat this. Look at that view. Look at this room."

MacLean filled two other flute glasses and held his up. "Still. Cheers?"

"Hang on," Sylvia said. Struck with inspiration, she set her glass aside and stepped away from the table. She reached under her hair and loosened the clasp that held her dress together.

Neither man said a word as Sylvia shimmied out of the little black dress. Vaughn bit his lip. MacLean ran his hand through his dark hair and then swiped it over his chin.

Stripped down to her lovely skivvies, Sylvia leaned against

the edge of the table. She reclaimed her glass and raised it in front of her. "Since we're not going anywhere, I figured I might as well get comfortable."

Vaughn let out a whistle through his teeth. "Jesus Christ, even in that little dress I had no idea just how much you've changed." His gaze took in every inch, his cheeks filling with color and his chest rising and falling a little faster with every breath he took. "You're just so . . . voluptuous."

"Amen, and cheers." MacLean clinked his glass against hers, and then Vaughn's, and took a drink.

Sylvia sipped her drink and suppressed a smile while the boys took big gulps. It was like she had lit a fuse by stripping down. While Vaughn seemed jumpy with impatience, MacLean had become tight as a drum. Whether he realized it or not, Sylvia could see that he was settling into an old pattern, simmering on the sidelines while she and Vaughn finished their champagne.

Grinning at Vaughn, Sylvia sauntered to the edge of the bed and sat facing MacLean and the floor-to-ceiling window. Vaughn joined her and leaned in closer for a kiss, but she moved just out of reach and held up her glass. "This is expensive stuff, you know. I want to at least enjoy the first glass uninterrupted."

Vaughn groaned. "Tease."

Sylvia ran a hand over his thigh. "Tell you what. For every sip I take, I'll let you take something off."

"Mine's already gone," Vaughn said. "I guess that means I need to catch up." He stood and started on his belt buckle. "Since we're not going anywhere."

She smiled up at Vaughn as he pulled off his T-shirt and revealed a flat chest speckled with reddish hair. When he was down to his briefs, she turned her attention to the other man. "What about you, MacLean? You're almost through with your second glass. You seem to have even more catching up to do."

He shrugged and put his feet up on a chair. "I'm fine over here. It takes me a bit longer to catch up."

"MacLean likes to watch, you know that," Vaughn said. Free from his briefs, his uncircumcised cock bobbed up. He huddled closer and ran his fingertips between her shoulder blades, down to unhook her bra. As the garment slackened, Sylvia shimmied the straps down and let the bra buckle.

"Baby, you're so soft now," he muttered, slipping his arms under hers and nuzzling the slope of her neck.

Her nipples hardened as he worked them between his fingers, sending hot little shards of pain throughout her body. As the heat of Vaughn's mouth sought hers, she turned her head to meet his tongue. For a moment, she felt suspended, captive in Vaughn's arms, while MacLean sat calmly sipping his champagne.

"Take another sip, Sylvia," Vaughn whispered against her mouth and dropped his head low.

Sylvia chuckled. "I can take a hint." She drank, and as the bubbly brew tingled in her throat, Vaughn nibbled along her throat. One by one, he unhooked her garters, but he didn't go for her stockings. Instead, he ran a hand along the inside of her thigh.

As she parted her legs and Vaughn stroked her through her panties, it became a little harder to breathe. She met MacLean's stare just as he was unzipping his pants. His lips curved into a smile, and he pulled his cock free of his boxers.

"Why don't you let me take care of that?" she said with a

grin, and sucked in a deep breath as Vaughn pinched her nipple between his teeth.

MacLean shook his head and slowly worked the skin surrounding his shaft. "You've got to put on a show for me first." His gaze dropped to where Vaughn's fingers hooked and pulled aside the lacy stretch of fabric covering her pussy.

Vaughn sighed. "And what a show it is. So wet . . ."

Sylvia held her breath and looked down. The liquid heat between her legs had streaked the length of her pussy, which was glistening in the dim light from the lamps on either side of the bed.

There was something about being displayed so openly, with all gazes upon her hot slit, that made the urgency of the moment unbearable. Vaughn, MacLean, her own stare, and even the open window: It was such sweet exposure.

Her clit throbbed as Vaughn circled his middle finger around its sensitive hood. With a soft moan, she started to tremble.

MacLean stood. In a moment, he was as naked as Vaughn and at her side, relieving her of the champagne flute. He drank down every drop and set the glass aside, then leaned over.

Both men worked to rid her of the damp panties and then hooked the mouths of her garters to her stockings again. Sylvia quickly freed herself of the corset. Only then did she realize why the garters had been reassembled: It was showtime. MacLean went to his carry-on, and from the side pocket, he produced a small videocamera with a flexible tripod. He set it up on the table and turned it on.

This wasn't the first time they'd filmed their reunions. Over the years, they'd amassed a small collection of videos to remember their time together.

"Lay back," Vaughn said as MacLean sat at her side.

Sylvia went back on her elbows and bent her legs at the knee. Like mirror images, the men flanked her and splayed one hand each on her plump thighs. Then they came upon her at once, each sucking and licking her hard nipples. Two sets of fingers probed her bare pussy: MacLean worked her clit while Vaughn penetrated her.

In unison, they set the perfect pace. A steady but powerful burn ignited, and she began to work her hips with increasing urgency. Through her moans, she could hear the wet sound of their mouths on her, and of their fingers working the slippery flesh between her legs. She was quickly losing the world around her to the fever rising beneath the surface of her skin.

MacLean lifted his head and met her stare. "Look at the camera when you come, baby."

As the delicious pressure quaked in her belly, it was such a struggle to stay upright, to keep her eyes open and focused on the little camera framed perfectly between her legs. Her moans exploded in tight little bursts as her lungs constricted.

MacLean's fingers worked the flesh-hood back and forth, back and forth, until she went feral, writhing and begging for release. Her clit throbbed. The walls of her pussy shuddered around Vaughn's fingers as sweet rapture flooded her. As the world continued to spin round and round, she flopped back. A low moan turned into a sultry laugh. She was drenched inside and out, and was barely lucid, barely aware of their fingers slowing as her heart kept pumping hot blood through her body.

Her smile faded as MacLean's shadow eclipsed her. While she had been surrounded by that delicious fog of afterglow, he had slipped a condom on. Sylvia took his hands and worked with him to move upright. The world spun around as he reversed positions, pulling her over him so that she straddled his thighs.

She glanced over her shoulder and found Vaughn with the camera in his hand.

"This is new. You're usually the first one at bat," she said to him.

He grinned. "I've mellowed in my old age."

MacLean ran his hands downward from her hips and cupped her ass. She turned her attention back to him as his fingertips kneaded into the soft flesh. Steadying herself with one hand on his forearm, she reached between their bodies and guided the tip of his cock through her slippery lips to the mouth of her cunt.

She had expected to be off balance and awkward with her extra pounds, and was surprised by how graceful the act was, just as it had always been. She sank down, and MacLean pushed up until he was balls deep.

A moan forced its way from the back of her throat, spilling forth before Sylvia could bite it back. She held onto MacLean's arms as he began to pump her from below. She led his hands to her waist and rocked against him, letting the friction build between his cock and her slick walls still throbbing from her earlier orgasm. Rings of pleasure pulsed along the length of her cunt. She opened her eyes to find MacLean seemingly giving in to the sensation, head tilted back and lips parted in a low groan.

"I can't wait for you to get a look at this," Vaughn said from behind, and Sylvia could feel the heat of his nearness. "Your ass looks amazing with that garter belt surrounding it."

Silent beneath her, save for the quick pace of his breathing, MacLean's grip tightened. The bed, the room, the whole damn world shook as he heaved against the mattress, pushing and pulling her, fucking her harder than ever.

With each stroke, the pressure between her legs built until it became unstoppable. She cut her nails into MacLean's hairy forearms and leaned forward to overtake him.

"Look at the camera, baby."

Through the mounting chaos of the moment, she thought it was MacLean who spoke in a growl, but it was Vaughn. He had moved to kneel at the edge of the bed with the camera in one hand; the other worked his shaft at the same pace with which she rode MacLean. Imagining herself perfectly framed in the small LCD screen, Sylvia leaned back and fell upon her hands to give Vaughn the most perfect view she could imagine.

The slight change in position evoked a series of eruptions inside as MacLean's shaft rubbed against her G-spot. Her abs screamed, and the backs of her thighs began to burn as she bucked faster and faster against him. She kept her eyes on the camera as long as she could until her orgasm pounded outward, flooding her with euphoria that took her breath away.

Her body went taut, and her inner muscles milked MacLean's cock. Sylvia looked down her body at him. His features contorted into a grimace, teeth bared and eyes squeezed shut. His grip tightened, and he surged up, his dick twitching as he emptied into the end of the condom.

From his place at the edge of the bed, Vaughn dropped the camera and leaned forward. He made a fist on the bedding, and in just a few more strokes he came, staining the opulent bedding beneath him.

The air in the room seemed too thin, and she struggled to

catch her breath. Vaughn flopped onto his side at MacLean's head. MacLean seemed suspended in a state between sleep and awake, his eyes open but glazed.

Sylvia shook off the last delightful ripple that ran through her and rolled away. "I think I earned a second glass of champagne."

As she filled someone's empty glass, she heard a chuckle behind her. She looked over her shoulder and found them both propped up and grinning at her.

"That, my friend, is pure cheesecake," Vaughn said.

"I couldn't agree more." MacLean reached for the camera and aimed it at her. "Give us your best Jayne Mansfield."

She half-turned her back to them and blew a kiss to each one. MacLean laughed, and Vaughn let loose with a catcall.

Sylvia brought the champagne glass to her lips and silently toasted her victory ass.

First Come, First Served

BY LOLITA LOPEZ

The jingling bell announcing the morning's first customer sent my heartbeat into overdrive, and a nervous flutter rocked my lower belly. I took a second to smooth my hands along the front of my bright yellow apron and to adjust the neckline of my V-neck tee. I glanced down at the girls to make sure they were perfectly displayed for my favorite patron.

"Good morning, Celia!"

The sound of Jay's low timbre made my knees weak. I turned and moved closer to the glass case filled with my special Mexican pastries. "Good morning, Jay."

"So what's new this morning?" He leaned an elbow on the glass and surveyed the day's offerings.

I smiled and gave him a rundown of the new pastries, and also pointed out some of his favorites.

Of course, Jay wasn't really interested in my baked goods. It wasn't just my hot buns that brought Jay into the bakery. It was also my big, beautiful breasts.

꧁꧂

High-flying movers-and-shakers like Jay Grant didn't usually make a habit of visiting this rundown corner of Houston's mostly Latino district. But for the past nine weeks, he'd walked through my door every day at 7:00 AM, on the dot, and greeted me by name. At first I'd assumed it was my deliciously sweet *pan de huevo* that brought him back morning after morning, but it quickly became clear he was interested in something that wasn't for sale.

I'd never had a customer who hemmed and hawed so long over choosing one of my heavenly delights. At first, I'd thought he was just one of those picky types. But soon, I noticed Jay always seemed to want to know about the pastries on the bottom shelf, or the ones tucked far into the corners of the glass case. That's when it dawned on me that every time I bent down, my very ample bosom was presented for his appreciative gaze.

I should have been outraged, maybe even disgusted. But for some inexplicable reason, I found it incredibly flattering that he drove halfway across town just to stare at my generous rack. Surely there were plenty of zaftig bakers and restauranteurs to ogle in his ritzy corner of the city. But, no, Jay came here. For me.

Honestly, I experienced an illicit little thrill every time I thought about it. I often wondered how prominently I figured in his personal spank bank. The very idea that Jay fantasized about me, about my lush rack, made me vibrate with excitement. Sometimes, late at night, after collapsing in bed from an exhausting day of work, I'd let my dirty mind run wild with visions of Jay stroking his big, thick cock and shooting his load right onto my tits. My fingers would slide through the slippery folds of my pussy as I furiously rubbed my clit and came hard with Jay's name on my lips.

Por Dios! What would my mother say if she knew those were the kinds of things that put me to bed with a smile on my face? She'd probably call me cochina, drag me to church, and throw me into a confessional booth.

⚮

"I'll take one of the gingerbread pigs and a pumpkin empanada."

"Sure." I bent forward slowly, making sure to thrust my breasts out as I grabbed a dark brown marranito and an empanada with the tongs. I plopped them into a small box stamped with my bakery logo and closed the top. "Coffee?"

He smiled that sexy smile that made my knees weak. "Please."

I don't even know why I bothered asking. By now, it was a given: large cup, a splash of milk, two sugars, and a couple of ice cubes to cool it down, so he didn't scald that sensual mouth.

I handed over his coffee and pastries, and our fingers touched briefly. A zing of electricity zipped up my arm. God, what would it be like to have his hands on my naked body, caressing my soft curves and intimate places?

"I didn't know you catered." Jay gestured to the stack of new brochures I'd set out the night prior.

"I'm trying something new. We get a lot of requests for large orders of pastries and breakfast tacos. I'm in the trial phase of adding a catering side to the bakery."

"You know, my firm does a lot of working breakfasts. Maybe we could do business?"

"Maybe."

"Let's get together tonight and talk about it. I'll cook dinner for you."

I marveled at how deftly he'd slipped in an invitation for a date. God, he was *good*. "Okay."

He grinned. "Great."

A swarm of butterflies went wild in my stomach as he jotted down his address on the corner of one of the brochures. When he handed over the brochure, our hands touched and lingered. His eyes glinted with the promise of what was to come. Sure, we were meeting under the pretense of starting a catering relationship, but I doubted very much we'd be inking contracts and swapping business cards at the end of the night.

He tossed a sexy smile and a wink my way before ducking out of the shop and to his sleek black sports car. As I watched him drive off, I started conjuring up all kinds of naughty scenarios.

And almost as quickly, I was assailed with thoughts of what needed to be shaved, painted, and primped before I popped up on his doorstep. I rapidly exchanged a series of text messages with my three best friends. "What should I wear?" I asked. The general consensus: something with a skirt that could be quickly flipped up over my head. "Panties?" Yes. Going commando just screamed *puta*, apparently. Eat something before I left the house, they said. Go easy on the alcohol at his place. Stuff my purse with condoms, and use them—don't take any of that "but baby it feels better without it" bullshit. Just in case, pack some supplies to ease a possible morning-after walk of shame.

I could barely concentrate all day. For the first time in months, I left the shop a few hours early. I had to get home and prepare.

That night, at a stoplight on the way to Jay's place, I used my rearview to touch up my makeup. My hands were shaking from excitement and anticipation, and I had to concentrate so as not to smear my lip gloss. So far, I'd almost missed an exit and nearly ran a red light. Not to mention I was so turned on I could hardly think straight. Already, my panties were damp. There was no controlling my raging libido once engaged.

As I stepped out of my car and handed over my keys to a valet, I felt seriously out of place. This was the hottest address in Houston's upscale condo market. It was the kind of place that screamed money and class.

At the lobby's front desk, a perky brunette directed me to a private elevator manned by a porter. (Apparently, to keep out the riff-raff, all guests were escorted. So much for taking my walk of shame in private!)

We arrived at Jay's floor, and I stepped out of the elevator. "Thanks."

The porter gave me a knowing smile. "Have a good night."

"I plan on it." My saucy reply garnered a shocked expression. I smirked and tossed my hair as the elevator door closed behind me.

I'd barely rapped my knuckles on Jay's door before it whipped open. Had he been listening, waiting, like some overeager puppy desperate for the return of his mistress?

"You look fabulous." His hungry gaze raked over my curves. "Red's a great color on you."

"Thanks." I felt silly as I blushed under his compliment. He looked devastatingly handsome in his jeans and blue dress shirt, the sleeves rolled up casually.

My insides were wiggling like a bowl of Jell-O as he ushered me inside his ultramodern abode. It was all gleaming wood and muted metallic tones. Nothing like the homey *Southern Living*-meets-Acapulco vibe of my place.

"Would you like a glass of wine?"

"Sure." I followed him into the kitchen, with its top-of-the-line appliances. My envious gaze moved around the spacious room as I placed my purse and a folder holding menus and boilerplate contracts on the nearest granite slab. "Something smells good!"

"Roast chicken and summer vegetables," he said, popping open the oven for a quick peek. Jay seemed surprisingly at ease in the kitchen as he fiddled with some kind of sauce reducing on a back burner.

"*Mmm.* Sounds delicious."

Jay gave a hum of agreement and poured me a glass of wine. I took the glass and inhaled the scent. I wasn't by any means a wine connoisseur and hoped he wouldn't ask any weird questions. Nothing made me feel smaller at parties than folks talking about the "notes" and "bouquets" of a particular wine. Unless I could see the label, I couldn't tell the difference between a syrah and a zinfandel.

As I sipped my wine, I became aware of Jay's suddenly pensive mood. He braced himself against the counter and played with the corkscrew. I could tell he wanted to say something but was afraid to open his mouth. "Is something wrong?"

Jay's mouth quirked to the side. "You know, I had this whole romantic evening planned for us. We'd have some wine and talk over dinner. I wanted to give you a great first-date experience."

"But?"

He dropped the corkscrew and took a step closer to me. The crisp scent of his cologne filled my nose. "But I can't stop thinking about what I really want to do with you."

I swallowed hard at his husky admission. "For what it's worth, Jay, I thought I wanted the same wine-and-dine experience, too. But now I'm not so sure."

"What do you want?" His voice sounded a bit shaky. The air between us practically sizzled with sexual tension.

I held his gaze. "You. Fucking me. Hard."

Jay grinned and teasingly asked, "On the first date? My, aren't we progressive?"

"Well," I murmured, toying with one of the buttons on his shirt. "This is more like a second date. I mean, the last nine weeks have basically been one long first date, right?"

Jay grinned and slid an arm around my waist, then hauled me tight against his chest. "I couldn't agree more."

When his lips crashed down on mine, I nearly fainted. If it hadn't been for his strong arm supporting me, I would have slid right down to the floor. His hand tangled in my hair as he devoured my mouth, his tongue stabbing between my lips. My senses reeled at the potent combination of man and alcohol exploding on my taste buds. I'd been kissed dozens of times before, but nothing—*nothing*—had ever compared to this.

Nine weeks of anticipating just what it would feel like to have Jay's lips on mine intensified the explosion of the moment when our mouths met. As he cupped my head in one hand, Jay allowed the other to slide down along the curve of my back to the full crest of my ass. He palmed a handful of my derriere and gave it a squeeze. The feeling of his hard cock stabbing into my soft tummy told me he appreciated a big juicy ass as well as big lush breasts.

His hand started to slip under the flimsy skirt of my red dress, but he stopped abruptly and broke away from our passionate kiss. "Shit!"

The second he spoke, I heard the telltale hiss of sauce boiling over and splashing onto open flames. He raced back to the stove and switched off the burner. But he didn't even bother to wipe up the sticky mess. Instead, he turned off the oven and pivoted back to me.

"That's going to be hell to clean up when it dries," I warned.

"Fuck it," Jay declared and took my hand. "Bedroom?"

"Yes, please." I snatched my purse from the counter and tried to keep up with Jay's long strides as we crossed the living room.

His bedroom was exactly as I'd expected: a low bed with a slate-gray headboard and crisp white bed linens. There was only one bedside table, and on it was just a lamp and an alarm clock.

"I know," he said, as if reading my mind. "It's not very warm and inviting, is it?"

I smiled reassuringly at him. "Different strokes for different folks, right?"

Jay laughed and tugged me close again. "You're something else, you know that?"

"So I've been told." I slid my hand along the back of his neck and pulled him down for another kiss. He growled against my mouth as he toed off his shoes. I followed suit, my mouth glued to his as I awkwardly reached down to tear off one slingback sandal and then the other. Jay chuckled as he bent down to match my strange angle and the jerky movements of my undressing.

When I started to lift my skirt, he closed his hand over mine. "Let me."

Nodding, I turned and presented my back, lifting my hair so he could reach the zipper. As if unwrapping a Christmas gift, he took his sweet time drawing down the zipper and peeling the dress from my shoulders. It fell to my ankles, and I stepped out of it.

Suddenly nervous, I crossed my arms in front of my body and hesitated. It was one thing when we were both flirting, fully clothed, but now, every ripple of cellulite and every plump, fleshy curve was exposed. I'd come to terms with the thick thighs and wide hips and megabosom years ago, but this felt different: Jay was the kind of guy who could have any woman. So what the hell would he want with lumpy, chunky me?

Jay pressed on my shoulder, nudging me to turn around, and I reluctantly spun to face him. He gently pulled my shielding arms away from my body and took a good, long look at me. "My god, Celia," he breathed. "Do you have any idea how beautiful you are?"

His gaze burned my skin as he studied my Rubenesque form. He circled me like a prowling cat, pausing behind me just long enough to unhook my bra and drag it free of my arms. My heavy breasts ached as they bounced free. My nipples were already pulled tight with arousal. Jay slid his arms around my waist and palmed my breasts in his big hands. I closed my eyes and leaned back against his chest as he caressed and tweaked and massaged.

When he nipped my neck, I shuddered and clenched my thighs. I could feel my pussy getting wetter and wetter. Then his hand left my breast and slipped into my red silk panties. I almost came when his fingers slid between my pussy lips and brushed across my clit. He turned my chin with his other hand and claimed my mouth again before dropping to his knees behind me and kissing the small of my back. He slowly dragged my panties down over my wide hips, his tongue gliding a path over my juicy apple bottom, his teeth nipping here and there and making me giggle.

He stood and moved in front of me. Taking my hand, he led me to the bed. Sitting on the edge of the mattress, Jay worshiped my curves as I stood before him. He buried his face between my breasts, then sucked and licked my nipples until my toes curled. I sifted my fingers through his short hair as he circled my belly button with his tongue and squeezed the plump cheeks of my ass.

Never, not once in my twenty-seven years, had I ever felt this beautiful, this wanted. Whatever doubt I'd held about Jay's possible attraction to me fled. Only a man who found me irresistible would lavish this kind of devoted attention on my curves.

Jay's eyes burned with lust. "I want you to ride my face."

The bottom dropped out of my stomach. I'd never had such a dirty request from a lover. My face flamed with embarrassment, but I couldn't say no. There was something deliciously kinky about the idea of sitting on his face as he tongue fucked my cunt. "Okay."

Jay rose from the bed and quickly undressed. His cock sprang loose from his black boxer briefs, which he whipped off and tossed aside. I couldn't help myself and reached out to stroke his erection. He groaned and sucked in a shuddery breath before pulling away abruptly. I was thrilled by the realization that he was *that* hot for me.

My belly flip-flopped with excitement and uncertainty as we climbed onto the mattress. He rolled onto his back and grabbed my hips. As he dragged me closer, the well-defined muscles of his arms and shoulders flexed. I tossed a leg over his waist and placed my knees on either side of him. With a little shimmying, I moved into place, my ass resting against his chest and my pussy poised mere centimeters from his mouth. His fingernails bit into the fleshy cheeks of my butt as he pulled me a little closer and dove into my cunt.

"Oh, god!" I cried out at the first flick of his tongue against my throbbing clit. It traced my slick folds and fluttered over my clitoris, then stabbed deep inside my wet hole. He sucked my clit between his lips and teased his teeth over the pulsing nub.

I'd never felt anything like it. My pussy was so open and exposed. Anytime I tried to pull away, his strong hands held me firmly in place. Jay showed no mercy as he ate my pussy like it was the most delectable dish he'd ever been presented. He moaned with enjoyment as he devoured my cunt and brought me closer and closer to climax.

I played with my breasts as my lower belly tightened and my clit buzzed. My breaths came in fast little pants. My thighs flexed and released as I chased the panicky sensation that heralded my orgasm.

"Fuucckk!" My body exploded with waves of pure bliss. My hips swiveled and rocked as I rode Jay's face. He urged me on and on, moaning excitedly and slapping my big ass.

Just as the first climax ended, Jay latched onto my clit again and forced another orgasm. The sensations his skillful tongue evoked were almost painful as he flicked and circled the oversensitive pearl. Part of me wanted to pull away, but most of me wanted to see it through. Jay's tongue slid slowly over my clit and picked up speed as my breathing changed.

When I came the second time, I shrieked and wildly pumped my hips. Jay's tongue seemed to be everywhere at once. There was no holding back the little gush that accompanied my mind-blowing climax. Once or twice, I'd squirted while playing with my vibrators and watching particularly naughty porn, but never with a partner. Goddamn but Jay was good!

Jay licked and sucked my pussy as if trying to swallow every last drop of the nectar he'd produced. Eventually, I couldn't take it anymore and fell off to the side. I ended up next to him, our arms touching. He wiped his shiny chin with the back of his hand, and I let out a loud belly laugh from the craziness of that orgasm. "That was fucking unbelievable."

Grinning, Jay pinned me to the mattress. He teased my mouth with a few sensual kisses, the salty taste and heady musk of my pussy heightening the intimacy of the moment. I reached between us and grasped his stiff cock. As I stroked him, I was reminded of my dirtiest fantasies. "Would you do something for me?"

"Anything," he whispered as he nuzzled my neck.

"Would you come on my tits?" I held my breath as I waited for his answer. When he broke into a wide grin, I knew I'd get exactly what I wanted.

"You dirty, dirty girl." Jay kissed me deeply, his tongue swiping mine. "Any particular way you want me to do it?"

I embraced my inner *putita* and decided to go for broke. "Do you have any lube?"

There was no mistaking Jay's enthusiasm as he nodded. He didn't even have to ask for directions. He knew exactly what I wanted him to do. I vibrated with eagerness and lust as he hopped off the bed, made a trip into the bathroom, and returned with a bottle of lubricant. He squirted some of the slippery liquid into his palm and worked it along his ruddy shaft. Another shot of the wet stuff went between my breasts. He painted my cleavage with the slick lube and then tossed the bottle aside.

"Do you have any idea how many times I've fantasized about this?" he said, moving into place, his knees on either side of my ribcage. "I've been dreaming of sliding my cock between these gorgeous tits for months."

"Sometimes, when I touch myself, I imagine your cock is right here, like this," I admitted. "I come so hard when I imagine your come splashing all over my skin."

I didn't know where the impetus for my shocking confession came from, but I couldn't help myself. I wanted—needed—Jay to know I'd rubbed out orgasm after orgasm with him in the starring role of my kinky fantasies.

I held my breasts together, compressing my cleavage, as he slid his cock into the fleshy tunnel and thrust back and forth. He took his time, rocking slowly as he enjoyed the sensation of my huge breasts hugging his erection. The expression on his face betrayed him. He was fighting for control. I licked my lips and whispered filthy encouragements. He fucked my tits a little faster, a little more forcefully. I pressed them together even tighter, increasing the friction against his sensitive shaft.

Even though we both wanted the moment to go on forever, the inevitable end arrived much too soon. With a pained growl, Jay pulled back and took his thick cock in hand. He stroked fast and furious as he shot hot jets of ropy white cum all over my breasts.

With every splash of the sticky fluid, my clit pulsed and throbbed. I held Jay's gaze as I rubbed his come into my skin and then licked it from my fingers. He groaned and fell onto the bed beside me, hauling me tight to his side. Content in my postorgasmic buzz, I snuggled close.

"You know," Jay said after a while, "this is a pretty good marketing technique for the catering side of your business. I'm ready to sign a contract right now."

"Hey!" I playfully slapped his arm and narrowed my eyes at his smiling face. I threw my leg over his waist and straddled his hips. My teasing wiggle seemed to awaken his recovering cock. I leaned down and brushed my lips over his. "Play your cards right and you just might earn a nice, fat discount. . ."

Small Packages

BY TENILLE BROWN

It had started with the newspapers. Then gradually, it turned into magazines.

Stretch had heard about it from customers, but he had wanted to leave well enough alone. When he saw somebody, one of his regulars, walk by with a new paperback tucked under his arm, he knew he had to put a stop to this thing. She was running a music store, and she needed to stick to that. Instead, she had started branching out, adding the morning paper, then the celebrity magazines, and now books.

That was *his* territory, and she had stepped over the line, directly into it.

Stretch's intent this morning was to tell her as much, but the tall, curvy structure of a woman walking past interrupted his thoughts. Coffee in hand, she strutted by, shoulders back, head high.

The sight of her made Stretch tell the well-dressed business-man in front of him that today's paper was on the house. It made him pull the shade down on his newsstand, put up his paper clock, and set it for an hour later. It made him leave his stand to go follow her.

The exact reason he followed her, he couldn't pinpoint. He could have easily waved or something to get her attention.

She hadn't seemed to notice *him*, though, standing there behind his newsstand.

But all she'd had to do was look over.

Stretch might have smiled, or winked, or something, just to keep her looking, though he never claimed to be a ladies' man. He knew he was no toad either.

Truth be told, Stretch liked what he saw in the mirror every morning. He had all his teeth, decent skin, an alright, though on the shorter side, build.

His hair—he liked that the best—was full and curly, and he could grow the hell out of a beard. He kept one, a full one, because it added years to his boyish looks, maturity to his youthful build.

Stretch was nobody's giant, but that was okay, too. Big things came in small packages; this he knew. But he wasn't one to brag.

But this one, she was a *big* package. She had wide shoulders and meaty arms. Two bags were slung over broad but soft shoulders.

Her breasts filled the lacy red cups that appeared now and then as teasers from the top of her spring dress. Stretch liked a woman who filled out her clothes.

Even her hair was big. Light brown and fitfully curly, it was piled in a messy heap on top of her head. Freshly fucked hair, it was.

Stretch licked his lips. This one was certainly woman enough for him.

Now, here he was, a few feet behind her on the sidewalk. Her maxi dress swayed. Her ass swayed. Stretch kept his eyes there.

He didn't know where the woman was going, but he knew he wanted to be there, too. He wanted to stand next to her and inhale, or get close enough for their arms to touch. He wanted to be the one standing behind her in a line somewhere in a place so crowded that he'd need to press against her soft and voluptuous body to make room.

But then she stopped on Main, in front of a record store.

The record store.

LOVELY'S, the pretty sign read. It was the store that was adding all that extra to its inventory, that was snatching the fiscal rug right out from under him.

The woman fiddled with her keys and opened the door. Since it was opening time and all, Stretch went inside, too. He watched the woman sling her purse aside and tinker around with the register.

Then the phone rang, and she snatched it up. "Lovely's," she answered. The name matched her voice; matched her wide, white smile. But her tone soon grew low and cold, almost a growl. Stretch thought he heard the words "not on your life" before she slammed down the phone.

"Well . . . can I help you?" she asked. Lovely, if that was her name, was talking to Stretch now—voice softer, but no less cold.

"I was waiting for you to open," he said.

Softer still, she said, "Oh yeah?"

"Yeah." Then he asked, "Crank caller?"

Lovely rolled her eyes. "Idiot caller. Been in the store before and thinks he can just call up for a date, like I'm hard up. You know how it goes." She leaned over the counter. "So, what are you looking for?"

Stretch almost told her . . . until he realized she was talking about the music. So he said, "A little Billie Holiday, if you have it."

Lovely cocked her head. "I have it all."

And Stretch already did as well, but he'd duplicate his entire collection if it meant getting next to her. He figured he could wait to talk about their little conflict of interest. Wait for a day when she was looking a little less sexy and he was feeling a little less horny. Maybe tomorrow, or the day after.

For now, Stretch took his Billie Holiday and a newspaper and slipped away.

<hr />

A week and three days of cat and mouse, and Stretch had yet to mention the inventory issue. Instead, he tried to impress Lovely by naming the tunes she had playing in the background. Lovely would try and stump him by changing it up now and then. She'd play some old, some contemporary. She'd play some jazz and some rock 'n' roll.

Customers came and left, but Stretch remained.

It seemed trite to ask if she had a man. And frankly, he was afraid of the answer. How could she not?

But Lovely did the talking for him. She asked, "Your woman know you're spending your time in here . . . stalking me?"

Stretch tried to measure his response. He didn't want to seem too quick or too eager. He said, "There is no woman."

Lovely looked at him, and her eyes seemed to be asking, *Well, what are you gonna do with a woman like me?*

Stretch liked that Lovely's confidence was big. That she was sexy, and she knew it.

"I'm gonna be straight with you, Stretch," she said finally. "You haven't been sniffing around here, buying music you probably already own, just for the hell of it."

Stretch said, "Okay."

"Okay, so what's the deal?"

And this was where he could have come out with it, but the thing of it was, she smelled so good, and her lips were so full and glossy, her eyes so big and bright, that all that came out was, "Well, Lovely, I—"

She put her hand up. "Let me guess. You want to fuck me, right?" She didn't wait for an answer. "Well, let me tell you something. My last man was a big guy. A perfect match for a woman like me. He knew what to do with all this." She let her hands roam over her well-formed body. "And if you had a little more meat on *your* bones, I'd give you the business in a New York minute."

"And I don't?" Stretch asked.

Lovely looked like she was considering it. Then she said, "Well, do you?"

"I'd rather show than tell," he said.

Stretch knew he could have easily redirected the conversation to the real reason he was here—why he had shown up here the very first day—but Lovely was talking again.

She said, "I'll tell you what. I'll give you ten minutes with me in the back, 'cause I think you're kinda cute. You do good in those ten minutes, I'll give you ten more."

Lovely was extending a challenge.

And the words sounded like they could have come from a blues record. Lovely looked like she could sing nasty blues, her full lips hugging a microphone like a cock.

Stretch was hard.

He ran his hand across his bearded chin. He didn't bother to tell Lovely that he wasn't a ten-minute man. He wasn't even a twenty-minute man. Of course, she would see that for herself.

Lovely locked the front door and turned the BACK IN TEN MINUTES sign around.

Stretch almost laughed.

They'd be back there until closing time if he had anything to do with it.

❧

Their bodies slammed against a box of CDs. Stretch went for Lovely's lips first. They were softer than he'd even imagined, and they accepted his with eagerness.

Her tongue was in fierce competition with his, wrestling with it until she had it under her control. And then she sucked on his so softly it left him weak.

Lovely's body was a winding road, and Stretch took his time getting where he was going. He liked the feel of fleshy thighs gripping his hips as he gave it to her fast and hard.

She was holding back, he could tell. She didn't want to give in, didn't want to burst after he had only been inside her a few minutes.

Stretch showed Lovely no mercy. He filled her with all she could stand, and gave her more, just in case a bit spilled over.

Lovely lifted her big, sexy legs enough to draw Stretch in deeper. She threw her head back.

Stretch ran his tongue along her throat. He couldn't resist caressing her ass, couldn't resist letting a finger find its way inside.

Lovely tightened around him at the surprise, then relaxed and became wetter still as his finger began to work her rear entrance while his cock sweetly tormented her center. Her body was pouring sweat. Her hair was matted against the sides of her face. Her peach dress clung to her golden skin. She was a beautiful mess getting fucked by Stretch, biting her lips and clenching her eyes shut as he thrust and thrust.

The sounds that came from Lovely's mouth were enough to swell Stretch to his fullest, so much he thought he might be a bit much for her, but she took it all, growling like a beast, her body glowing like the sun.

Lovely sucked in air between clenched teeth just before she came, and then she flowed, hot and thick like lava, around Stretch's pulsating cock.

He gave her no reprise, he just held her steady as he fucked her. He talked nasty in her ear as he bounced her against him, enjoying every drop of her postorgasmic wetness.

When he was close to coming, he released her carefully in a sweaty heap on top of the box. He jerked his cock as she watched, mesmerized, and he came intensely on her exposed thighs.

Lovely placed her hands there, rubbing, almost as if confirming that the last half hour had actually happened.

Stretch touched Lovely's shoulder, then her cheek.

Before he left her there.

❧❀❧

Around the corner at his stand, Stretch liked thinking about the fact that Lovely was spending the rest of the day attending to her customers while she was sopping wet between her legs. That while they were talking to her about Gillespie and Springsteen, she was thinking about how Stretch's cock had swelled and throbbed inside her walls just moments before.

❧❀❧

Lovely was wearing white today, a sophisticated, button-down shirt dress with a silver chain belt that hugged her waist and made Stretch think about dark rooms and Lovely being chained to a wall wearing latex that barely contained her curves.

The fitted dress was unbuttoned dangerously low, her heavy brown cleavage peeking over the top. Her belly, soft and round, pressed against the crisp fabric.

Stretch looked away, because if he didn't, he would have surely been staring.

Lovely sold a few CDs while he pretended to browse the aisles.

Stretch waited until the store was empty except for the two of them, then he leaned across the counter and, in a bold move, ran his finger across the exposed skin of her cleavage.

"Have you been thinking about me?" he asked.

"You wish," Lovely said. "What are you trying to prove, anyway?"

"Nothing," Stretch said, "I don't have an Apollo complex, my dear."

"And I'm not your dear," Lovely said, frowning.

Word for word, she had a response for him. But Stretch had the key, he certainly did, and he knew what could quite literally bring Lovely to her knees.

"I want to give you head," Stretch leaned over and whispered in her ear.

Lovely couldn't stifle her smile.

"What?"

"You heard me. I want to eat you out."

"Fine then. Just let me turn my sign."

Stretch held up his hand. "No, no. No sign. I want you right here, right now."

"And my customers?" Lovely asked.

Stretch tested her. "Big, strong woman like you . . . are you scared?"

Lovely cocked her head to the side. She looked him up and down. "Hell no."

Stretch circled the counter and walked up behind her. He gave her plump ass a nice feel of his solid thickness.

His chest against her back, he could feel her pulse quicken, revealing that Lovely was excited—and maybe a little scared, too.

Stretch reached both arms around her waist and let his hands fall to the front of her and meet at her middle. His hands met in a diamond, pressing firmly against the wispy fabric of her dress. Lovely was moistening her panties, and the dress as well.

Quickly, and without warning, Stretch pulled the dress up to her thighs, and then again, just as swiftly, up around her wide, round hips.

He rubbed his cock against her ample ass, teasing her so sweetly that her soft body quivered.

Stretch could get straight to business, and he knew it, and it would be such sweet relief for her, being bent over the counter, her face pressed against the glass as he pressed inside of her.

Instead, he crouched, and, on bended knee, he parted her thighs. He felt her heat on his face as he drew nearer. Then he snatched down Lovely's lacy panties. In one swift movement, he tore the fabric from around her thighs.

Lovely's pussy was exposed, fuzzy and plump, like an apricot, and when he placed his tongue between the folds, he found that it was just as bitter and just as sweet.

Stretch whispered into Lovely's wetness, "If you can stand ten minutes of me kissing your pussy, I'll give you ten more."

And what began as a giggle from her lips became a whimper. Her thick thighs weakened and trembled against his cheeks.

Stretch dug his fingers into Lovely's hips, holding her as still as he could, but she was strong, and her body tried to pull away from the sudden explosion of pleasure. She was strong, but Stretch was stronger, and he kept her there, where he needed her, his face pressed between her thighs, kissing and licking. He wouldn't move until she was coming in his mouth, mashing her pussy violently against his lips.

Helplessly, Stretch reached down. He hadn't thought he would need to, but he did. He released his engorged cock from the confines of his pants. Once free, he began massaging himself and licking Lovely's pussy simultaneously.

"Are you—" Lovely started, then, "oh my . . . you're . . ."—because she could hear the slick sliding of Stretch's hand over his own cock, could feel the motion of his hand working on his shaft.

Stretch's groan against Lovely's pussy caused her to raise up on her toes.

The bell over the door sounded.

Lovely gasped, but Stretch didn't so much as pause.

"Let them carry on," he whispered, pulling only slightly away from her cunt. And carry on they did. He heard footsteps head toward the back of the store.

"Let's see how silently you can come."

"Um, um," Lovely managed breathlessly.

Stretch whispered, "Oh, you will come. I'm not stopping until you wet my mouth."

Her body slumped in surrender.

And Stretch sucked harder; licked faster, rougher. He worked vigorously on himself.

Lovely was a six-foot-tall vibrator when she came, and Stretch wasn't far behind—wetting his palm, her calves, and the floor, all at once.

He pulled her dress back down, and Lovely straightened it.

Stretch waited until the customer paid and left before he stood up, smacked Lovely on the ass, and walked from behind the counter and out the door.

Lovely stood there, and she didn't seem upset, or even surprised.

She just asked for a paper and thumbed through a magazine.

Then she said, ever so sweetly, "I hear you have a little problem with how I'm running my business, sir."

Stretch said, "Oh, really?"

"Next time," Lovely said, "you should talk to me."

Stretch nodded.

Lovely added. "We should get together sometime and talk about vendors. I know where you could get a deal."

And Stretch could have said "Alright." He should have said, "Okay," and left it at that.

But he pulled down the shade on his stand, turned the corner, and followed Lovely down the street.

Decadence

BY SATIA WELSH

Just as Victoria ducked under the awning of Decadence—the restaurant she had both discovered and fallen in love with nearly six weeks ago—the clouds opened, and the rain poured down.

She smiled to herself, acknowledging her good fortune that she'd made it to the restaurant before the downpour. *It's about time I had some luck,* she thought. The blind date she'd just escaped from was the worst she'd ever been on. As a consolation, she'd decided to head to her favorite place to indulge in some of her favorite food.

As she moved toward the front door, she slowed to a stop. An old woman, bent over a walker, her head wrapped in a multi-colored scarf, was moving toward the entrance. Victoria smiled at her and stepped back to let her pass.

That's when she noticed the handsome young man holding the door open for the old woman. He'd mistakenly thought Victoria's smile had been for him, and he smiled in return, letting his gaze roam over her, obviously enjoying what he saw.

It was why she had chosen this—her favorite dress, a saffron-colored silk two-piece—to wear this evening. The top portion was snug around her bust, lifting and presenting her girls very nicely, and the skirt wrapped perfectly around her lower body, flaring out at her waist to fall just above the knee, accentuating all of her glorious curves. For a touch of elegance, she had pinned up her long, chestnut curls.

Though foremost on her mind, from the start of this evening, had been getting her brains fucked out, that hope had been shattered when her date turned out to be such a nightmare. Still, she was above seducing this young man, who was obviously out to dinner with his grandmother. Even if he was hot.

Inside, it was considerably emptier than Victoria had anticipated, especially because of the crowd that had been milling around outside. She glanced at her watch. Ten o'clock . . . but it *was* Friday night.

Off to the right, yet another good-looking man in a chef's coat stood speaking to two middle-aged women. From her previous visits, she recognized him as the owner and head chef. *Hotties everywhere,* Victoria thought. *Everywhere but on that horrible date I just escaped.* The chef looked up after a moment, his blue eyes finding hers. She inhaled slightly at the intensity she found in those eyes.

When Jack saw her standing there, so lovely and curvy in her form-fitting yellow dress, he found himself frozen. (Well, except for the physical heat he was feeling.)

It was her—the one he had been secretly watching from the kitchen for the last six weeks. Every Tuesday she came in, at about nine o'clock. She sat alone at a back corner table and relished every bite of food that came from his kitchen. Her expressions, her beautiful smile, even her body language suggested that each bite she brought to her lips was a tiny celebration. Her enjoyment of the food hinted at unbridled passion under the surface.

Still, he was a little surprised that he was so fascinated by her. He had never been interested in anyone her size. It wasn't that he found full-figured women unattractive. He desired confidence most in a woman, and he hadn't met many large women with much confidence—especially around food, his chosen profession and his life's passion.

This woman was different. Every movement of her body screamed confidence. And she virtually dripped sensuality.

He couldn't help excusing himself from his customers, and as he sauntered over to her, his gaze never left her beautiful full figure. He could see right away that she gave as good as she got: Her gaze—both tempting and teasing—boldly took in his athletic, lean build.

When Victoria saw the chef walking toward her as if hypnotized, she had to fight to hide a triumphant smile.

"Can I help you?" His voice was rich, pleasant.

"One, please?" She heard the hope in her tone and tried not to blush.

"I'm afraid we're closed tonight for a rehearsal dinner. The sign was posted on the door." His tone wasn't chiding, merely informative.

Victoria smiled slyly. She hadn't noticed the sign, because she had been more taken with other things at the entryway. Glancing around the quickly emptying dining room, she nodded toward the two women he had been speaking to. "Then why do those poor women you were talking to look so sad?"

"The wedding was called off by the groom when he found out his bride-to-be was having an affair."

"Ouch," Victoria said, wincing. "Guess my night could have been a lot worse." She turned her smile on him. "There's just a little thing I was hoping for."

Jack's eyes dropped to her neckline, lingering over the flawless, pale skin of her lovely cleavage. "And what is that?" he asked with just a hint of suggestion.

"I have just come from the worst blind date of my life. All I want right now is a cigarette. But I quit six months ago—which is, incidentally, when I found your restaurant—so I can't have one. I was hoping for a piece of your French silk pie instead."

Jack smiled. "Well, since I certainly can't refuse a loyal customer, you are welcome to sit at the bar. I've sent my entire staff home for the night, but I've still got some cleaning up to do. Would you like some coffee?"

Victoria grinned. "Only if you put Bailey's in it," she answered saucily. "By the way, my name is Victoria."

"Jack." He took her outstretched hand, bending slightly to kiss the top of it, keeping his blue eyes locked on hers. The kiss sent sparks up her arm, and she shivered deliciously.

⚬❦⚬

Fifteen minutes later, everyone except for Victoria was gone.

Jack went to lock the doors and returned to the bar, where he had served her a piece of his French silk pie, only to find she hadn't even taken a bite yet. Refilling her coffee with Bailey's, he said, "Aren't you going to eat it?"

Victoria seemed to flush slightly. "Sometimes I enjoy the anticipation."

Jack's dick tightened at the innocent remark. He suddenly imagined her blindfolded in bed, waiting for him.

She looked up at him, her eyes earnest. "You make the absolute best food I've ever tasted."

It was Jack's turn to flush. "I'm glad you enjoy it."

"'Worship' is more like it." Victoria picked up her fork and sliced through the whipped chocolate and cream.

As she lifted her fork, she eyed it as if it held a piece of heaven. Her eyes closed before it was in her mouth. Her movements were languid; her lips pouted as she slid the fork off them, empty. Her jaw moved slowly, savoring the decadent flavors exploding in her mouth. Before taking the next bite, the tip of her tongue dipped out to capture a dab of whipped cream.

It was nearly Jack's undoing. He white-knuckled the bar, imagining her going down on him with that same expression on her face. He took a deep breath to compose himself.

When she opened her eyes again, he excused himself. "I'll leave you to it then," he said and left.

⁂

Victoria tasted another bite as she watched him walk away. *My, but he has a cute ass.*

But she couldn't make much more headway with the pie. After two cups of coffee with Bailey's, the pie seemed a bit too rich. But she was going to need a takeaway box, because she would definitely be finishing it by the end of the night.

She hopped off the barstool and made her way toward the kitchen.

The swinging doors were closed, and she paused to look through the circular window. Jack stood in the middle of the kitchen, putting trays of uneaten appetizers away. He worked quickly and efficiently. His chef's coat made it hard to appreciate all his muscles, but the short sleeves allowed a fabulous view of sinewy, muscled arms. And his hands. For a moment, Victoria let herself wonder what they would feel like on her body, caressing her nipples, rubbing her clit, grabbing her hips as he fucked her against the walk-in cooler door.

Victoria flushed again—this time without a hint of embarrassment. The images alone were making her wet. She needed an orgasm badly. Obviously, she was probably going to have to go home and give one—or multiples—to herself. *If only I'd had more to drink, some liquid courage,* she thought. She didn't think two coffees and Bailey's would lend her enough nerve to march over to Jack and rip his clothes off.

Or could it? She squared her shoulders and pushed the door open.

⚘

Jack was pulling his dinner out of the Salamander broiler above the oven when he saw Victoria approach. Though he was genuinely surprised to see her, a devilish, knowing smile escaped his control.

He put the hot dish on the wooden island just as she stopped before him. Her nose twitched slightly, and then her eyes discovered the source of the aroma.

"Are those stuffed mushrooms?" she asked, and Jack chuckled at her rounded eyes and her look of anticipation.

"Yeah, my dinner—left over from the rehearsal. Would you like some?"

She nodded enthusiastically, and Jack pulled out two forks. "Be careful, the plate is extremely hot."

Victoria stuck a cap with her fork, pulling the whole thing out. She turned it over like a lollipop and began to blow on it.

Jack nearly groaned, watching her. He didn't know how this woman made eating such a sensual act, but it was driving him a bit crazy.

As soon as it had cooled down, Victoria gave him a triumphant look and popped the whole little cap in her mouth. Again, her eyes had closed as she took the first bite. She moaned, and her body began to sway slightly as she chewed slowly. A delighted sigh escaped her, and her eyes came open.

Jack couldn't restrain himself any longer. *What's the worst that could happen? A knee to the balls? It was worth it.* He took a step toward her, taking her upper arms. "I'm *really* glad you like it," he said, and covered her mouth with his.

For the briefest moment, Victoria froze, and Jack worried he had made a mistake. But then she dropped the fork, wound her fingers through his blond hair, and started kissing him back. Jack's left hand cupped her cheek, while his right snaked to the small of her back, pulling her to him. He tore his mouth from hers, kissing a trail to her ear.

"Do you have any idea how sexy you are eating my food?" he said huskily in her ear, then suckled her earlobe. She shuddered in his arms. He continued down her neck, inhaling her lovely scent as he went, pausing to bury himself in her abundant décolletage. She smelled of milk and honey, and faintly of vanilla. He ran the tip of his tongue over the top of her breasts, along her silk neckline, and he heard a soft moan escape her lips.

God, he wanted her so bad. He spun her around, pushing her back against the island. Her body was so soft against his as he pressed himself onto her. He wanted her to feel him, to feel how hard he was, and he rubbed his denim-encased dick hard against her silky skirt. Victoria gasped loudly. Almost too loudly.

Jack stilled, wondering if he had hurt her. It was his downfall —his passion—and sometimes he got too caught up in the moment. "Are you okay?" he asked. Victoria looked confused for a moment. "I didn't hurt you, did I?"

Victoria shook her head. She grabbed his collar and started pulling him back to her. "Not at all. That was a *good* gasp. Don't worry about me, sweetie, I'm not going to break." Her eyes twinkled. "Sometimes I even like it a tad rough."

Jack groaned as he pulled her into a crushing kiss. She met his passion head on, body moving against his, hands roaming over him. He kissed down her neck again, but this time went farther. He knelt in front of her, his hands going to her waist.

He rested his forehead against her navel, letting the warmth of his breath seep through the material of her skirt. Slowly, he let his hands move down her hips, slightly cupping her ass, then down the back of her stockinged legs to rest at her ankles. He heard her inhale slowly as he made his way back up the outsides of her legs, up under her skirt. He paused halfway up her thighs.

He gazed up at her, smiling. "Garters?"

Victoria smiled back, giving a slight shrug. Jack slowly pushed her skirt to her knees, savoring the unwrapping of a delightful present. He hooked a finger through the white lace of her thong, pulling it ever so slightly to the side. He bent his head and kissed her clit.

Jack heard Victoria's air leave her in a rush as his mouth began to taste and tease her. He used his fingers to spread her shaved lips, his tongue swirling and sucking. Her hips started to rock against him, angling to give him more access. She dug her fingers in his blond hair, pulling his face into her, moaning deeply. But when his finger slipped into her wetness, she flung her arms wide, braced back against the countertop.

With his left hand, Jack cupped Victoria's ample derriere, pulling the bottom half of her body greedily to him. Her whole body moved in unison with his, undulating sexuality. He lifted her right leg over his shoulder and heard her groans as his tongue replaced his finger, delving deeply into her while his thumb worked her clit. She was sweet, tasting of mangos and her natural muskiness. Jack groaned himself as he switched again, his tongue flicking her nub and his finger penetrating deep inside of her. He felt her muscles contact around his index finger. Her hips jerked rapidly, fucking his face and hand.

"Oh god," she breathed.

Jack didn't stop, though his hard cock strained painfully at his jeans. He desperately wanted to bury his dick inside her and feel her cum around him. Almost as much as he wanted to feel and taste her cum on his face. And she was close. . . .

Boom!

The loud crash of a door stopped them both. Jack heard his name shouted and realized it was his sous chef, coming in from the back. He quickly stood, pulling Victoria's skirt down. For a moment, he thought she would panic. But her brows merely rose in question. His groin tightened even more when he realized she didn't seem to mind they had almost been caught.

"It's my sous chef. I'll get rid of him. Can you meet me across the hall in the banquet room?"

Victoria straightened her skirt. "As long as you don't dally," she said, hips swinging as she walked away.

Victoria walked through the kitchen doors and found the entrance to the banquet room almost directly across from her. Her panties were soaked, and the wet lace pulled across her tingling clit as she made her way to the carpeted room. The banquet room was large and was still set up for the canceled rehearsal dinner. The tables were adorned with white tablecloths and red roses, though they hadn't been set with any dinnerware. Victoria made her way to the front dais, where the bridal party would have sat.

Feeling a bit wicked, and wanting things to pick up from where they had left off, Victoria carefully unzipped her yellow skirt, letting it fall to the floor. She slipped out of her thong panties, realizing that at this point they were just getting in the way. She undid her top and took it off, feeling the air on her exposed skin. Then she reached up and pulled the pins from her hair, letting her long, chestnut hair cascade around her.

She knew how gorgeous she looked, how the corset she wore hugged her waist, serving up her décolletage like Jack's French silk pie. She stood proudly on the raised dais, in front of the long, white table, her legs wide, hands resting on her hips.

When Jack entered the banquet room, he nearly stumbled when he saw her. Her eyes met his in a challenge. Then he started toward her—reaching her in three long strides—and grabbed her and pulled her to him, kissing her fiercely. Victoria could taste herself on his lips and was even more turned on. She felt the table on the back of her legs, and on the front of her leg, she felt the length of him through his jeans. When his mouth left hers for the top of her breasts, she was panting. *Alright, enough is enough*, she thought. *I want him now!*

His fingers fumbled along the top of her corset. It was a true corset, lacing up in the back only, without any hooks in the front or side to make it easier to get out of.

"How do I get this damn thing open?"

She chuckled at the frustration in his tone. "The laces are in the back." She took advantage of his distraction to pull down his zipper. Her mouth made a satisfied sound as nine inches of hot, hard cock fell out. She took the length of him in her hand, pulling him toward her spreading legs.

❧❦❧

Jack sucked the air through his teeth as her warm hand wound around him. He tried to still himself and braced one hand on the table, next to her ass. He had almost just cum at her touch. Astonished, he shook his head. He hadn't been this out of control since college. Now she was trying to take him inside of her, but he knew if he entered her, it'd be over in a matter of seconds.

"Not yet," he managed to say. He took her by the hips and turned her around so that her ass was facing him. Victoria seemed to like that. She wiggled her ass. "How did you know this was my favorite position?" she asked breathlessly, then pressed herself against him.

Jack groaned. He pulled away just far enough so that he wouldn't enter her. He needed to get control of this, or he was going to embarrass himself. He didn't think he had ever wanted anyone more. His fingers deftly loosened the top of the corset so it stayed in place while her ample breasts fell forward into his waiting hands.

❧❧❧

Victoria moaned as his large hands kneaded her breasts. He was rubbing her nipples between his thumb and forefinger, just the way she liked it. She stood straight, then reached over her head, and back behind her, until her fingers found his hair. She thrust her hips back against him, fucking the air, while he kissed the back of her neck, her spine, her ear—all as he teased and pulled her nipples. She was vaguely aware when one of his hands left her. Then she heard the ripping of foil and was thankful he had the foresight and sense about him to use a condom. Frankly, at the moment, she didn't give a damn.

She leaned forward, elbows propped on the table, and felt Jack's hands slide the length of her body to her hips. She still wore her wedge sandals, and they tilted her backside up in invitation. Victoria's heart raced. She needed him to pound into her, fast and hard. Instead, as he held her hips, Jack, with agonizing slowness, slid the entire nine inches into her dripping, hot cunt.

Victoria came. Her mouth opened, though no sound escaped. Her body arched up as it tensed. Jack held her as her body shook and her muscles convulsed around his shaft. And as her lungs began to work again, she dropped gently forward toward the table, and he began moving inside her.

She moaned. His thrust quickened. Almost instantly, Victoria felt anther orgasm beginning to build. His hand went up the length of her spine. She pushed up from the table, palms down. Her breasts bounced back and forth as they rocked to his thrusts, her nipples brushing the white linen tablecloth.

"Yes," she gasped in encouragement, wanting more. His pace was still steady. Victoria pushed back, meeting his thrusts. She needed more. She needed it harder. And faster. She reached her hand around, nails digging into his hip. His body circled around hers, his rhythm a constant. His hands found her nipples again; they were ultrasensitive from her first orgasm. Victoria jerked at the contact, a line going from her nipple to her pussy yanked taut.

❧❧❧❧❧

Jack felt Victoria's body contract violently, and he stilled. "Did I hurt you?" he asked.

"No!" Victoria said and slammed back into him, taking his cock inside her to the hilt. "Harder!" She pulled forward and slammed into him again. "Faster!"

For the third time that night, Jack nearly came unexpectedly. He really hoped she meant what she said, because after that, he wasn't going to be able to control himself. His fingers dug into the soft flesh of her hips and plunged into her. Her wet, deep pussy took every bit of him as he pounded into her. Victoria grabbed the white tablecloth, apparently trying to steady herself against his hard, quick thrusts.

"Harder," she groaned.

Jack's fingers twisted into Victoria's long hair at the base of her neck. He wrenched her back by the hair, firmly but without yanking, forcing her to arch her back. Victoria called out as another orgasm took her. Her legs shook, but Jack didn't stop. It felt too good. Her muscles squeezed him as warm wetness flowed down the front of his balls. He turned her head to kiss her, not letting go of her hair. He pumped into her, pulling out to the tip of his dick and slamming back into her.

"Don't stop," she gasped.

"I can't," he said. And it was true.

Still holding her hair, Jack wished he had more hands. He pounded her, his flat stomach slapping her ass. His palm came forward to circle her nipple and he felt her shudder deeply. He knew she was going to climax again . . . and so was he. Harder and faster, he fucked her. His hand snaked down her front till his fingers slid to her swollen clit.

"Yes!" she screamed as another orgasm washed over her. Jack let go of her hair but caught her around the middle before she could fall forward. He pulled her back, so that she was flush with his chest, his cock ramming into her one final time. He cried out as he came with her.

❧❦❧

As Victoria came back down to earth, Jack held her tightly. Eventually, he slowly eased out of her, then left to dispose of the condom. She artfully reached behind her and tightened her corset. It still wasn't perfectly in place, but it would keep the girls in till she got home. Jack came back and collapsed in a chair directly in front of the dais. Victoria watched him, her hip cocked up on the table. When their eyes met, she gave him a smile like a cat that had just got the cream.

"I do believe that was better than your French silk pie," she mused, then moved across the room to where she had left her clothes.

❦

Jack watched Victoria walk over to her pile of clothes. He loved how proud she was of her body. So sexy. He admired her curves as she bent at the waist to pull her skirt up around her, giving Jack one last look at her glorious ass. He felt himself stiffen. He realized to his surprise he wanted her again. Right now.

She zipped up her skirt and moved to stand between his legs. She bent again at the waist, this time granting him a nice view of her front. She kissed him lightly on the lips.

"See you Tuesday. Regular time?" she said, and dropped her wet thong onto his hard cock.

Already anticipating next week, Jack watched her sashay from the room.

Excuses

BY NINA REYES

I'm trying hard not to stare at him. He's leaning against the granite counter, so relaxed and cool that he looks like nothing has ever bothered him. He's not supposed to be my idea of a fantasy, this skinny poet kid who took James Dean's careless lean. Snatched those eyes, too. I want to tell him to get the fuck out. I also want him to bend me over the counter and fuck me as hard as possible. It appears I'm at an impasse.

"So, Maya, when you're not housesitting, what do you do for a living?" he asks under those eyebrows of his. Only now do I realize I hadn't said anything for a few minutes.

"Well, I'm getting my BA in journalism right now," I tell him in a low, husky voice. "So I'm working in retail right now." I make the words louder this time, more clear.

Jonathan nods and takes two steps toward the refrigerator. As he bends down to examine the contents, I take the opportunity to check out his ass. Nice. He's thin—thinner than what I usually go for—but there's something there. Not completely flat, thank goodness. When he straightens back up, I make a show of examining the ends of my braids.

"Is that how you met Lily? At the boutique?" He has a carton of orange juice in his hand. His free hand begins twisting the cap. They're philosopher hands. Long fingers with slightly knotty joints. Tidy nails, tinged slightly pink.

I toy with the increasing pile of mail collecting on the table, trying to get the edge of each envelope to line up just a bit more. "Yeah. Just after she married Daniel. The rest is history."

Jonathan lifts the carton and begins to part his lips. I put an end to my fidgeting just long enough to loudly clear my throat, cross my arms, and raise my eyebrows.

He stops before his mouth touches the carton. Understanding reaches his brown eyes a split second before that smile makes a reappearance on his face. He places the carton down on the counter and begins opening cabinet doors.

"You're good," he says. "I give you that."

I watch him open and shut a few more doors while I blush slightly at the compliment. I want him to whisper that in my ear. I shudder thinking about his mouth so close to me. His mouth traveling down my body and tasting me everywhere. I look down at my jeans. Tight around my wide hips and thighs. I'm not wet enough to soak them through—yet.

After a few tries, Jonathan finds where the glasses are kept. He pours the orange juice with a dramatic flourish. That half-smile reappears, and with a fast wink, he empties the glass of its contents.

Once it's gone, he gives a satisfied sigh and begins refilling the glass. "And that's why Daniel trusts you to keep watch over his lovely abode. His devil-may-care brother might just kill a house-plant or commit some other terrible crime."

I laugh, despite myself. "I'm sure the life of the cat was also placed under consideration."

Both corners of his mouth go up this time before he takes a small sip from the glass. Everything is quiet, and I have no idea how to continue. I opt to put my hands into my jean pockets. What little pocket there is, anyway. Women's jeans aren't designed for function. They only serve to invoke the tears of hapless shoppers and to make me wonder exactly how big my hips and thighs look at this very moment.

I have to sound casual. "So if you're so devil-may-care, what made you stop by at nine o'clock in the evening?" Casual enough. Maybe.

After a particularly loud gulp, he responds, "I finished a job not too far from here, and I knew they'd left sometime in the last couple of days, so I decided to come by and make sure every-thing was all right." He sips again while using the other hand to lean against the counter. "Unbeknownst to me, they already have someone working the case." Lifting his eyebrows in a conspirato-rial way, he finishes the glass and moves to place it in the sink.

"Daniel said you're a photographer." I make myself leave the relative comfort and security of the dining table to step into the entryway. He's either interested in me, or not. "Are you working on something in particular?"

"Ah, you know, just this advertising thing. Some girls and some products. You know." I couldn't tell if he was being evasive because he didn't want me to wonder about his evenings, or if he was really that blasé about it.

"That sounds exciting. What, a bunch of sexy girls draped over cars or something?" I sound like I'm joking, but I'm on a fishing expedition. I wonder if he's ever fucked anyone outside of his race. Hell, I wonder if he's fucked anyone built like me.

He gives a low chuckle before responding. "Yeah, something like that."

Fuck you, skinny, hot photographer. You probably eat models for lunch. I don't let the sentiment show up on my face. I walk another step closer. "Sounds exciting."

"Really it's not. I don't get to pick the subject matter, and you can only shoot oiled, bikini-clad women so many times before it starts to get boring." He pauses for a moment before lowering his head and raising his eyebrows. "Despite beliefs to the contrary."

I bite my lip to keep the laugh in, but my face gives me away. Busted.

That half smile comes back. "Hey, it's a paycheck. It affords me the ability to take the pictures I want on my own time."

"Like what?"

"I don't know. Like you?" His head's low, giving him a shy, bashful look I can't possibly buy.

Still, I walked right into that one. "You can't be serious."

"Why not?"

He's serious.

"Come on," he says, and before I can say anything, he grabs

my hand and leads me into the living area. His equipment is by the front door.

"This is crazy. What, curvy black women are in short supply in your line of work?"

Already on the floor assembling his camera, he stops what he's doing long enough to give me a look of pure shock. "You're black?"

It takes me all of two seconds to realize he is completely fucking with me. Now I can't stop laughing.

"Much better." The megawatt smile is back. Camera ready, he gets to his feet and begins walking around me in circles. The prankster falls away, making room for the professional photographer instead.

With the camera aimed in my direction, my nerves hit. "What do you want me to do?" Immediately, I realize it's a loaded question.

He lowers the camera. "Lean on the arm of the couch for right now." He's staring at me with purely artist's eyes. Nothing but business. I appreciate the fact that he's capable of respect—except respect isn't exactly what I have in mind.

I sit on the arm of the couch and begin taking his directions: "Sit straight . . . face relaxed . . . right hand up . . . tilt your head." He moves right and left, like a pugilist in the ring.

Arousal begins to take hold of me. I like him ordering me around. The camera flashes blind me, making me feel momentarily helpless. My pussy is getting wet. My nerves begin to settle down. I lift my tits and chin up farther. The smile on my face becomes genuine, reaching my eyes.

He makes a thumbs-up sign. I let him take a few more pictures before I make my move. I grab the bottom of my shirt and lift it over my head. Unlike the lower half of my body, my tits are demure—though still showstoppers when encased in black lace.

It stops Jonathan in his tracks. He pulls his face away from the camera just long enough to look at me before snapping more pictures. Another pause. He looks me in the eye and asks, "Can you lift your left arm up and bring your hand behind your head?"

My arm goes up, and I smile.

The flash keeps going off. My nipples harden in response to the attention. I decide to up the stakes. I stand and undo my jeans. Despite my impatience, I pull them down slowly, like I'm unwrapping a gift for him.

Again, he stops and stares. He licks his lips. I step out of the jeans, never taking my eyes off him. I'm on display. I own this. I demonstrate my dimensions by taking my hands and running them down the sides of my body. The wide curve of my hips. Wearing nothing but a black-lace bra and panties.

To my satisfaction, he gives a little sigh. I can see his jeans bulging outward. *Good.*

"Turn to the side."

It's not a request. My ass, the subject of many comments and conversations, is now in full relief. I make the decision to stand there in pride. I crane my neck to look at it myself.

"Stay there! Just like that. Please." His hand is up, palm out and fingers splayed.

I look down and smile. A blush spreads across my face. I put my hand across my heart to steady the beating before I arch my head and get back into position.

The flashes come faster than ever. My panties are soaked, and I want nothing more than for Jonathan to fuck me. I want to feel his cock. Feel him fuck my mouth. I want to sit on his face. I want to know what he can do with that clever tongue of his. A shudder runs through me, and my breathing starts to become uneven.

The flashes stop.

"Why don't you touch yourself?" he asks, eyes roaming my body.

I hesitate for a moment. It's dangerous to have pictures of yourself in such a compromising position. But I want to be dangerous with him. I want him to take me to the edge.

I sit on the arm of the couch so I can face him. My hand starts playing with the edge of black lace. Fingers work their way down. My middle finger finds my clit. Short, light strokes just to start. My shoulders round forward, and my breathing becomes more sporadic.

A click causes my unfocused eyes to look up. Jonathan is still behind the camera, intent on documenting me fucking myself. The thought sends a pulse through my pussy, and suddenly, I need more. Another finger begins to explore the wet slit. I'm almost panting now.

The camera no longer has my attention. I only have eyes for the hard-on in his jeans. On the other side of that zipper is something I've only been able to fantasize about until now. I lick my lips. "Take it out," I tell him.

After a few more clicks, he lowers the camera until it's almost hanging from the strap around his neck. His face still has that serious look, though one eyebrow is slightly raised. "You want to see my cock?"

Hearing him say that causes a shudder to run through me. I gather enough focus to make coherent sentences, though I refuse to stop fingering myself. "I want to see you work yourself over. Jerk it." I let myself smile wickedly.

The corners of his mouth turn up slightly. Letting the weight of the camera rest against the top of his stomach, he brings a hand to the zipper. He lowers it. Slowly.

Bastard.

Now I have a finger deep inside of me, caressing the walls of my pussy. The heel of my hand is applying pressure to my clit. I want to come so bad, but I want to see more of him first.

Finally, he reaches inside his pants and pulls his cock out. I'm staring at the light purple head, and it's all I can do to keep myself from closing the last few feet between the two of us and putting my lips around it. My fingers continue working instead, though I can't keep myself from giving a small moan.

He smiles at that and starts sliding his hand along the shaft. Putting on a show for me. I slide a second finger into my hole and continue massaging my insides. I'm entranced by his beautiful hand running up and down his dick. He's putting a bit more force into it; I can see the muscles in his arm working. He's still holding back a bit, probably intent on driving me to the edge of insanity.

My self-control isn't up for it. Fuck this. Turnabout is fair play. And with that, I let the last of my modesty fall away. I lift my right leg up so my foot is resting near my ass and my knee is level with my chest, giving him an unobstructed view of my glistening fingers deep inside.

It works.

Two big steps is all it takes for him to close the distance and grab me. Those long fingers wrap around my upper arms, pulling my face toward his. His lips press into mine, the taste of orange juice filling my mouth.

I have to put my leg down to keep myself from falling. My wet hand is holding onto his arm for support. He pulls me to my feet, pushes me in front of the couch, and turns me around.

Arm around my waist, he plants his lips on my neck. He smells like soap, with a bit of sage. My eyes close, and my back arches, pressing my ass right into his crotch. His dick feels hot against the side of my ass cheek. I let my hand wander behind me so I can feel him. Suddenly, a hard shove forward. Now off balance, I have no choice but to put my hands along the headrest. My back arches, raising my ass farther in the air. My vision is limited to the seat of the couch. I have no idea what he's doing.

He takes the opportunity to run a hand along the side of my body. A hand reaches under my bra and begins to knead my breast. Fingers pinch my nipple. My body is on fire. I push the lower half of my body in his direction. *Please fuck me. Please.*

The hand moves away from my tits. I start to twist my head around to make sure everything is all right, and then I feel the tips of those incredible fingers lightly stroke my hips. They trail to the back of my thighs, tickling me, before sliding up my backside. He proceeds to grab either cheek. Not difficult. There's more than a handful there.

"This is just . . . lovely." A light smack emphasizes his point. I arch my back farther. I'm beginning to lose my mind. I'm about to tell him as much, but then my panties are slid down to my knees. My pussy is nearly dripping now, and I can feel the heat of his cock near my thigh. A moan escapes my lips. It turns into a cry when I feel the head of his dick play at the wet heat of my entrance. I push back in an attempt to envelop him, to swallow that rigid flesh and fill the aching void inside of me. He backs away.

God damn you.

I hear him chuckle softly. I am on the verge of being pissed. I reach back blindly, attempting to grab him. One of his hands rests firmly on the center of my back. The other grabs my wandering fingers. He holds my hand gently.

"You don't handle teasing well, do you?" he asks in that humorous purr of his—the one I found so endearing all of twenty minutes ago.

I open my mouth to give him a piece of my mind, but then his hand falls away, and the head of his cock begins to massage my seeping hole once again. Nothing leaves my mouth except for a loud hiss.

"Yeah, I like that, too," he says. He's smiling right now; I just know it.

"Please," I whisper. My knees are starting to shake.

"What?" he asks, feigning innocence.

I'm finally willing to ask for it. "Please fuck me."

His hand softly trails the line of my back before coming away and smacking my considerable ass, hard this time.

"You know, you're really beautiful, Maya."

Before I can say anything, his cock sinks in. He puts it in to the hilt on the first thrust, forcing a yell out of me. I feel him start to slide out and then come back in again. Out again, to the head, only to come back in. The pleasure is so deep, I can't keep myself from bucking against him.

The hand keeping my upper body in place moves; both hands are now on my hips. He's controlling me, invading my cunt with well-timed strokes. I push back, attempting to match each of his thrusts. He gives a loud, shaky exhale before increasing his speed. I can't keep up with the little bit of leverage I have. Instead, I close my eyes and give in to the sensation of being thoroughly fucked.

His hips pound against me at full force. Each time his body slams into mine, my flesh reverberates. I rock my hips and ass, altering the placement and depth of his cock. I hear him groan loudly, almost loud enough to drown out my unladylike grunts. His balls slap against me, and it feels absolutely delicious.

Adjusting my balance, I rest my upper body against the seat so I don't have to hold myself up. My ass is completely in the air, getting ridden hard. I bring a hand to my swollen clit. I rub furiously. My nerve endings fire and pop. I can't think, I'm so close now.

His grunts are matching each thrust. We're both close. Suddenly, I feel a finger probing my asshole. Massaging. It's a completely new sensation. Between my clit, the thick pressure in the walls of my pussy, and feeling yet another hole being filled, I start to come—fucking hard. My body spasms, and I buck. I want him to fuck all the way through me. I don't exist anymore. I'm only an ass and a pussy, radiating pleasure and heat.

His last few thrusts are so hard, it almost hurts, making it even more wonderful. Somewhere in the middle of my frenzy, he came as well. Our bodies are still while regular breathing is reestablished. I feel him exit, leaving my body. I mourn the loss of him.

There's a quiet thump. I raise myself and turn a bit. My back protests, and I know I'm going to be sore in the morning. Inside and out. I look down to find Jonathan laying on the floor, still panting from his exertion. One hand is resting dramatically over his forehead.

"You dead?" I ask, as I begin to crawl down to join him.

"Very much so." His breathing is getting softer.

I rest my body against the line of his, feeling his heartbeat regulate. The smell of sex seems to be everywhere. All body fluids and desire. I place my hand on his chest, brown skin on white. My eyelids begin to feel heavy, and then I come to a sudden realization. I sit up.

"Jon?"

"Mmh?" he asks, raising his head slightly.

"Those pictures of me—particularly the ones of me, you know—those aren't going to see the light of day, right?" My voice is nonchalant.

He snorts and lays his head back down, a Cheshire Cat smile plain on his face.

"Right?" I hear the register of my voice go up.

"Darlin', I ran out of film long before then. No worries." He chuckles before placing both hands behind his head, looking too confident by half.

"Bastard." I lay my head on his chest. I don't want him to see my smile.

"You just needed an excuse, and I just so happened to have one."

I lightly slap his arm. He slaps my ass in return.

"Yep, an excuse. A reason to fuck me silly. The camera was just convenient." Even though I can't see his face, I know he's still wearing that damn smile. I give an exasperated sigh.

"Well, don't worry," I tell him. "I won't need one in the future."

Recognition

BY SALOME WILDE AND TALON RIHAI

Molly Bauer—call her Moll—shifted with a groan in the cramped seat beside Gate A76 at the Detroit Metro Airport. The seats weren't exactly skimpy, but what was the point of the armrests? If people were sitting next to her (and no one was right now, because it was nearly ten o'clock at night, and all but two of the flights had taken off), they wouldn't use the armrest, and she wouldn't use the armrest, and so the armrests would just act as separators that made sure everyone knew they had personal space. But unless you were scrawny, there was no personal space.

And Moll wasn't scrawny. She was ample. An ample woman who liked being ample. She liked the way her ass filled a chair (when it wasn't an uncomfortable airport seat), and she liked the way it filled a pair of jeans. She liked her big lap, and the way it was perfectly filled by her small, but not scrawny, lover, Michelle (call her Shell—except don't, because it was over, for good this time).

Moll's hands were big and strong as she dug through her backpack for the apple she knew was there, somewhere in its messy depths. At last she found the juicy red prize, rescued it from between the little stuffed cheetah she never traveled .without and the wrinkled copy of *Popular Science* she'd bought for the fossil cover story but would likely never read. She held the apple up in the fluorescent light. It shone encouragingly. She began to toss it, gently. There was something reassuring about tossing an apple and catching it. And, as she waited for the plane that would take her back to Atlanta and the apartment where Shell would most assuredly not be waiting, reassurance was a good thing. That she tossed it only three times before it dropped to roll across the aisle and between the feet of a fellow traveler, however, was not reassuring.

⚜

While pulling her carry-on behind her with one hand, and smoothing her unruly hair with the other, Rhiamon Adabelle Davis (no, not Rhiannon; yes, she's sure) mentally replayed the highlights of the judo tournament that afternoon. She'd taken a hard-won second place, and she had enjoyed preparing for the event, wearing her lucky *gi* and the belt that was given to her by a fairly famous judge, back when she was just beginning. She could still remember how proud she'd felt when she'd been gifted the special belt after she'd worked so hard to earn her rank.

Rhiamon liked to work hard. And she liked being big, capable. She liked the way her body did what she told it to do—whether it was on the tatami or in the bedroom—and she smiled to herself as she wondered if Amy missed her.

Though she liked her body, her hair was another matter. She wished she had the guts to just shave it all off. The kinky mess was disobedient, even in the tight braids she often forced it into. That day, she'd braided her hair for the tournament, but now that it was over, she'd taken the braids out, letting her scalp relax. To keep her hair from her face, she wore a brightly colored headband. She shrugged off the knowledge that her grandmother would give her an earful (Rhiamon's ear gripped tight in that strong, black hand) about going out in public looking like *that*.

Her thoughts were interrupted when a big, bright apple rolled to her feet. She'd almost bent to pick it up, but before she could it was being retrieved by a large hand and a muttered "Excuse me."

In that instant, Moll's eyes met Rhiamon's, and the power of recognition struck them both like a blow to the chest. It was not the stuff of romance, for Moll liked her women on the femme side (which the traitor Shell was), and Rhiamon preferred hers of the petite, sporty variety (which described her new girlfriend, Amy, perfectly). Rhiamon took in the ample Moll as Moll took in the capable Rhiamon. Both new and yet familiar, each saw a reflection of herself. And it was good.

Certainly, there were as many differences as similarities between the two, from skin tone to coiffure. Where Moll was as pale as her distant German ancestors, Rhiamon was a rich, mixed-heritage tan. As Moll peered up at the mass of golden-brown curls and matching eyes, Rhiamon took in a startled hazel gaze beneath a short, spiky crop of sandy blond.

But this was surface difference. The real truth was in the twin bodies—in big ass and small chest, in broad shoulders and big hands, in thick legs and strong arms.

And if Rhiamon was looking forward to Amy's touch and Moll was nursing her wounds and waiting for her next girly-girl, you wouldn't have known it by the way Rhiamon extended her hand to pull Moll up from her knees, or by the way Moll took it. With a firm grip and the fruit of temptation between them, how could they not wait out their layover together?

❧❧❧

"Atlanta," Moll answered when asked, polishing the already shiny apple on her jeans.

"New York," Rhiamon replied, confirming that they were indeed headed in opposite directions.

"Judo tournament" met "visit to an aging aunt." Tales of overpriced apartments flowed. A toast was made to the inevitability of unsatisfying jobs. Names were shared, but not those of Shell and Amy.

When Moll at last bit into her apple, she found it as sweet and crunchy as its gleaming exterior promised. Then, unthinking, she held it out. As she watched Rhiamon unself-consciously turn the fruit and take a bite just beside hers, she knew the exchange of pleasantries had become something else altogether.

As Rhiamon's teeth crunched into that apple, recognition gave way to a flash of unexpected desire. She chewed and watched Moll closely.

Moll watched Rhiamon with equal, wordless intensity, and when the airport loudspeakers suddenly blared, reminding them to never leave their baggage unattended, the two of them jumped.

Rhiamon laughed. A decision clicked. She tossed the apple to Moll, grabbed her carry-on handle in one hand and Moll's backpack in the other, and walked across the dirty carpet—knowing, just knowing, Moll would follow.

✦❧✿❧✦

The lightness of Rhiamon's laugh was a siren's call. Moll found herself allowing the stranger to take hold of her belongings without complaint. She took another bite of apple as she rose and tagged after the voluptuous ass in its camo cargos, wondering if she, too, looked that good from behind. Though they were likely only headed to the little bar to fill the minutes before their separate planes took them in separate directions, Moll was thrilled to be led somewhere new. She flipped the half-eaten fruit into a trash can along the way.

Rhiamon saw the bar but passed it by. That was not her destination, not the indulgence she sought. Instead, she led the way to the restrooms, striding confidently past the echoing, U-shaped,

WOMEN'S entranceway, to the smaller room, labeled FAMILY. She opened the door and pulled Moll in behind her, then turned the lock with a satisfying click. Fighting the urge to giggle, she let go of her carry-on and Moll's backpack. Then, pushing the other woman up against the door, she closed the space with a kiss. *Is this what I feel like?* she wondered as her large hands grasped ample hips and her mouth sought reward in reciprocation.

⚜

Moll had no time even to gasp as she returned the kiss and reached around to tighten the embrace. How surprising to have to extend her arms, to realize she could not get all of that abundant ass in her grip. *Is this how it feels to hold me?* The lips that pressed against hers were full and soft, and she deepened the kiss with heart-pounding abandon. Maybe everyone who spends time waiting uncomfortably in airports has a bathroom-sex fantasy, but how many indulge? A soft grunt of pleasure escaped her as the heat of Rhiamon's mouth met her own, as tongues wrapped and hands clung and eyes squeezed deliciously shut.

To Rhiamon, Moll's mouth tasted of apple and the mint of sugar-free gum. Moll's hands were strong on her ass and made Rhiamon's pussy tingle and moisten. Moll's skin was soft, and her flesh was soft, even as muscles moved beneath the dips and roundings her hands found as they moved up beneath Moll's shirt, over her waist and belly, to her chest. Her breasts were handfuls, just like Rhiamon's own—though Moll's resided in cups, and Rhiamon's were held close by a sports bra. She felt hard nipples and pushed the fabric up and away, so she could roll them between her fingers and feel the gasp it brought. Then she ground her hips against Moll's even as Moll's hands tugged her closer. Pulling her mouth away, briefly, she kissed down that creamy neck, nibbling and sucking as she kneaded Moll's familiar-feeling breasts.

The urgency in Rhiamon's searching fingers and tongue made Moll's wet slit clench. She let her head drop back and felt the bathroom wall cool behind her. When, she wondered, was the last time someone else took control of her like this? Hands in a mass of cloud-soft hair, she guided Rhiamon's mouth to her exposed breast and groaned as she began to suck. Her voice echoed in the small room.

So soft, Rhiamon thought, as the hands in her hair insisted she move her head down and suck a crinkled nipple into her mouth. They knew what they wanted, those hands, and weren't afraid to get it. Rhiamon grinned around her mouthful of tit, her hands sliding down to Moll's waistband and back up again as she treated the other breast to the same. So different from the gentle touches and breathy moans she was used to, but so recognizable.

Moll's fingers tightened in Rhiamon's hair, then moved down over her shoulders and arms. She couldn't resist squeezing and fondling as she went. Suddenly a muscled bicep was sexy, a fleshy forearm was delectable. She arched into Rhiamon's mouth as she reached around to shove her hands into the back of the tight waistband. The sweet mound of her ass was warm and dense and yielded deliciously to her grasp.

Rhiamon's mouth came off Moll's chest with a gasp as fingers met her ass. It was a tight fit, and she reached down and unbuttoned her cargos with a flick and a zip, and then, with a little more difficulty, leaned to repeat the same maneuver with Moll's jeans. Discovering that Moll wore boyshorts with dancing alligators on them was a delight, second only to her discovery of Moll's ass. She grabbed it and pulled her tight. She was breathing heavily and nearly blind with desire. But who needed to see, with such a pliant ass in her hands? Rhiamon groaned as her fingers flexed and stroked, moving down to caress big, defined thighs, and moving back to the front, feeling Moll's jeans slip a little as she did so.

Moll was not to be outdone in the groping department. Rhiamon had gotten to her breasts first; now she was determined to make first pussy contact. Her eyes flickered open a moment to catch a glimpse, in the mirror, as she shoved down Rhiamon's pants and saw the soft stripes of what she was certain, from personal experience, was a size 24 Lane Bryant double-string bikini. As cargos and panty gave room for more play, Moll quickly reached around to get a hand between those golden thighs. It was ridiculously awkward, but somehow, that just made it hotter. She stroked the patch of neatly trimmed pubic hair and parted the plump labia to find a lush, gratifyingly soaked treasure. She curled her middle finger and slipped it just inside to moisten it, then rubbed up the wet silk of inner lips to a clit tucked within a tight little hood. A rich, heady scent drifted up, strong but sweet, and her mouth watered for a taste.

Fingers inside her panties, underwear, whatever. Rhiamon could never decide what to call them, and what did it matter, when Moll's fingers slid between her lips and stroked her very, very hard clit? Instead of grabbing control, for the moment, she merely made a breathy grunt of consent and pushed into the touch as her hands gripped that sweet ass and her mouth moved to cover Moll's once more.

Moll's fingers and tongue were each exploring a different site of drenched heat. She hoped she was giving as much pleasure as she was getting as she broke the kiss and bent to draw her teeth against the shirt she should have been patient enough to lift. She grazed and tested until she found the nipple beneath layers of clothing, then bit—just enough to be felt—and held.

Rhiamon was pretty sure she made a surprised sound, but she was more sure that she gushed around Moll's fingers. Her nipples and clit seemed equally hard, and her own scent always aroused her. In reciprocation (or retaliation), she moved one hand around to slide down Moll's belly and into the low-cut waist of her well-filled boyshorts. Her fingers found surprisingly soft curls, and though she couldn't be sure, she'd bet they matched the ashy blond of Moll's hair. It was unusual to find a girl who didn't shave or wax (Rhiamon did both) but the lushness of what seemed to be an entirely natural, downy bush was an incredible turn-on. Her fingers made their way through the hair until she found wetness, and then she dragged her middle finger along the slit.

Just as Moll gave a low grunt at the way Rhiamon's rush of wetness now coated her fingers and palm, she gave another, louder one at the invasion of her panties. "Fuck yes," she muttered, releasing Rhiamon's nipple to rise and claim her mouth as she turned her hand and put her thumb to work on that clit while taking the risk of thrusting two fingers into the sopping core, hoping against hope that Rhiamon liked penetration as much as she did.

"Ahhhh ohhh fuck!" Rhiamon rejoiced at the feel of thick, nimble fingers inside her. Moll definitely knew her way around a pussy. Her voice was loud, but she didn't give a damn; she never did when she was getting her grind on. She put her mouth back

to work, latching onto Moll's as she slid her finger into Moll's folds to find her sensitive places. Every woman was different, but Moll's big pussy was so like her own, the plump lips and full mound. Her labia were prominent, and her clit hood ample over a very hard clit. She smoothed the growing wetness around as she moaned into Moll's mouth and ground against that big hand. In about two seconds she was going to slide into her "dirty talk" zone, she could feel it coming.

Moll pumped her fingers as their kiss grew deep and sloppy. She ground into Rhiamon's hand, helping her to find that little spot just at the left of her clit—there, just there! They were devouring each other's moans, fucking each other with hungry hands, pressing tightly together, forcing the world to hold still for them so they could pitch over its edge. As Rhiamon found and held her clit captive, Moll raced to climax with shocking ease. With what little mind she had left, she made herself release that juicy ass to slip up Rhiamon's shirt and fight her way under the tight sports bra where she squeezed a ripe little peach of a tit.

Rhiamon jerked at the grip, tossing her head while her hair tried valiantly to escape the headband. As Moll thrust into her, Rhiamon pulled from the kiss to let loose a string of profanity whose highlights included "Yeah, fucking take my fingers," "You know you want to come, baby," and "Harder, harder, harder, fuck yeah!" She drove her finger deeper into Moll's tight cunt (for it had magically transformed from pussy to cunt in her mind as her arousal and need grew), feeling it clench around her as she stroked the sweet spot on her clit and felt it swell harder. Moll's fingers seemed to know exactly where her trigger was, because she could feel climax building between bursts of dirty talk and wetness that was soaking not just Moll's hand, but her own panties and thighs as well. The combination of rubbing and fucking that spot deep inside her was bringing her home, hard and fast.

Moll felt the telltale flush rise from nipples to throat as Rhiamon's delectably foul mouth drove her arousal up and up. She humped and rubbed, shuddered and groaned. When she heard herself crying out, "Please, oh god, please!" in a voice whose desperation she could barely recognize, she knew she was lost. She clung to Rhiamon's breast, demanded her fingers to keep working, held her breath, and felt every muscle in her body tighten for the blast.

"Fuck, yeah," Rhiamon all but hissed. She shuddered hard but drove her fingers harder, panting as she felt Moll stiffen. Knowing she was about to tip over the edge loosened her mouth further as she murmured—or maybe shouted, "That's right, give it to me. Give it *all* to me." Moll's fingers didn't stop moving in and out of her pussy, and Rhiamon didn't stop grinding, and her body was suddenly hot from her scalp to her cunt as she reached the height of sensation and shot up to peak fiercely, intensely, into the cascade of gushing and writhing satisfaction. She rode it out, hard, wringing every scrap of pleasure from Moll's hands and mouth, as Moll took pleasure from hers, squeezing her finger rhythmically as she whimpered and shook.

As orgasmic cries gave way to panting and mutual shudders, Moll returned to the present enough to grasp the words that were coming over the loudspeaker. "This is the last call for Delta Airlines flight 2233 to Atlanta, Georgia. All passengers should be aboard the aircraft at this time." She gulped, swallowed, and stared, disbelieving, at the disarrayed stranger who had so unexpectedly given her such a remarkable gift. "I . . . my plane," she stammered apologetically, pulling her shirt down and fastening her jeans, then bending to grab her backpack. Unable to find more words, she leaned in to kiss Rhiamon's soft, parted lips. "Thank you." There was no time for more. As she grasped the door handle, she wondered dizzily whether she should ask Rhiamon to hurry after her, to jot down her name, a phone number, an email address. She turned, looking deeply into the wide light-brown eyes with their climax-heavy lids. "Thank you, Rhiamon," she said, needing to hear the name in her mouth just once.

Rhiamon moved slightly to give Moll room to hurry and get her pants up, gather her things. She didn't want her to miss her flight, after all. The last, soft kiss tingled on her lips, and she smiled as she buttoned her own pants. "It's okay," she said when Moll paused, obviously hesitant to kiss and run, but it was clear this was the only option. "Go on, Moll." Her voice was throaty from the pleasure and exertion and, yes, afterglow.

The moment she heard Rhiamon say her name, Moll knew it ended here, and knew why. This shared experience, this powerful moment of recognition, was not the foundation for something more, but was its own reward, its own moment in time. She smiled, nodded, opened the door, and ran. Mind hazy as her legs carried her to the gate, she turned one last time in the direction from which she'd come, as the attendant scanned her hastily retrieved boarding pass.

Rhiamon adjusted her clothes and took a minute to pull her headband off and put it back on properly before exiting the bathroom to watch Moll dash for her gate, backpack and bottom bouncing. It was a gorgeous sight. When Moll turned, Rhiamon raised her hand and waved, just a little, still smiling, hoping Moll could see her, hoping she could see her smile. Hoping she would smile, too. As her hand came down, she smelled Moll's scent on her fingers and brought them to her lips.

Moll echoed Rhiamon's wave, a final smiling reciprocation, and dashed down the ramp to the plane. Her pulse was still racing, her nipples and fingertips tingling. She tried to replay the encounter from beginning to end; it was for now just a beautiful blur. Absurdly, she wished she still had her apple, and she fought the mad desire to run back to the garbage and retrieve it. But she had something far better than forbidden fruit, she mused, as she made her way to seat 14C. She had replenished confidence in her own desirability. Who knew, maybe her next girlfriend would be a judo champion.

Passing the Time

BY GWEN MASTERS

"I wish you would talk to me," she said. "I need to know."

Amber was looking in the steamed mirror, bending close to the glass, her hands on the sink in front of her. "If you don't want me, say you don't. Don't make me wonder."

She shook out her thick hair and stared into her own blue eyes. She was more than a little concerned over quite a few things, and the way her boyfriend was acting lately was on the top of the list. Their normally good sex life had taken a nosedive, from once a day—or at least once every few days—to nothing in well over a week. Not even the slightest sexual innuendo had come from him.

Tonight she had wondered, for the first time, if he had lost interest in her. Whatever was going on, she didn't think it was her fault. Things had suddenly changed, and try as she might, she couldn't pinpoint the reason.

She kept looking at herself in the mirror, critically now. She saw a woman who weighed a bit too much, a woman who was starting to look closer to thirty than twenty. Her eyes showed signs that far too many tears had been shed over the past week.

But those eyes were a deep, jeweled blue. Her lips were full and soft. Her hair was a classic shade, gorgeous and all natural. Her body might have a little extra padding, but it was strong enough to surprise most men, especially when she was riding them hard in bed, holding them down, with her hands on theirs.

"And let's not forget my sterling personality," she said to the woman in the mirror. The woman didn't reward her with a smile.

Amber sat heavily on the side of the tub. The house was silent, save for the low hum of the refrigerator. She wondered if the phone would ring, and then remembered that she had gotten in the shower at one in the morning, hours after he should have called her. Of course he wasn't going to call her in the middle of the night. He was probably sound asleep, having forgotten to call. Had he really forgotten about her?

Amber dried her body with a vigor that left her skin aching. She marched into the bedroom and grabbed the lotion—the really good and expensive bottle of white cream he had given her. The scent was classy, understated. She needed to feel feminine right now. She bit her lip in concentration as she squirted the lotion onto her perfectly smooth legs.

Her skin was soft enough that she didn't really need lotion. She used it anyway, remembering how he put it all over her with his broad, strong hands. She loved those rough, calloused hands, the ones that worked hard to make a living. There were only very good things to be said for men who were broad of shoulder and strong of body. She thought of his voice, how smooth it was, the way it sounded like rough gravel when he was tired. He had been tired quite a bit lately.

Why was he so tired? Was it the work at the factory? Or was it something else? Amber closed her eyes and shook her head hard, trying to throw the negative thoughts from her mind.

She smoothed the lotion down her legs and then rolled onto her belly. She smoothed the white cream over her arms as she thought about the changes in their relationship. She hadn't been doing anything differently. She had made it clear how much she wanted him: as often as possible. She knew he needed reassurance, and that he wasn't the kind to ask for it, but she was the kind to give it without needing a request to do so. She had been faithful to him since the day she met him, months earlier. She had gone out of her way to make him feel wanted, needed, and loved.

She felt loved. She knew that he loved her—knew it as clearly as she knew she would take her next breath. But the *needed* and *wanted* parts were the ones she was having trouble with.

"He wants me; he wants me not," she chanted as she pumped the top of the lotion bottle. The white cream curled into her hand, and again, she thought about sex with him.

The sex was pretty damn good. Some of the best she'd ever had, truth be told, and she knew it was mostly because their communication was so open. She had no problem telling him what she wanted, and he was more than happy to oblige. She loved doing what he wanted and needed, but he rarely allowed her to focus on that. He might be one of the few men on earth who meant it when he said that her orgasm was just as satisfying to him as it was to her. It had taken time for her to believe that, but believe it she did.

It had taken time for her to get used to his constant teasing, too. All the man thought about was sex—wait. That wasn't exactly true. Not sex. *Intimacy*. He loved the closeness of the act, all parts of it: before, during, and after. He was the only man she had ever met who could outpace her in sexual imagination—and that was saying something very significant indeed.

She had all sorts of ideas now, and no one to share them with. She wondered again where he was, and why he hadn't called, like he said he would.

Leaning over with a sigh, Amber put the lotion on the windowsill above her bed. As she did, her gaze landed on the space beside her nightstand.

On the little red box peeking out from under the bed.

In that box resided a variety of adult toys—everything from vibrators to dildos and from pearls to clamps. She looked at the box for a very long time. In all her worry lately, her sexual desire had taken a vacation. She had played with herself the day before and found that the resulting orgasm wasn't worth the time. It was nothing but a thin, joyless spasm of physical release that left her feeling even worse than she had before she started.

But as Amber looked at the box, she started thinking.

First she got sad.

Then she got angry.

Then she got busy.

She yanked the box out from under the bed. Something in there rattled—batteries, probably. She opened the top and looked at the first toy there: the dildo that looked quite a bit like her boyfriend's cock. She picked it up, testing the weight of it in her hand. She looked at the phone. It sat there silently, mocking her hopes that she would hear his voice, while she contemplated exactly what she was going to do with that toy.

Because she was going to do *something* with it, by God.

Something kinky.

She closed her eyes and took a deep breath. The plastic had warmed in her palm. It still didn't have the heat her boyfriend's body did—what could?—but it would do in a pinch. And if this wasn't a pinch, she didn't know what was.

Her hand drifted down her chest. Her nipples were hard and hurting already. She ran her hand along where he had been, traced the bruise his tongue and teeth had left there a week ago. She shifted in the bed, lay down on her back, and let her fingers walk all over her skin. It was slick from the lotion, warm from the shower. Goosebumps rose everywhere when she thought of the kisses he had bestowed on the back of her neck, of the way he had kissed her ear and made her sigh. She touched all those places and then some, and hardly realized her other hand was moving up and down on the toy in long, fluid strokes.

Her legs shifted. Her knees opened. She slid one hand down between them, careful not to touch the most sensitive places. She loved the way her legs felt. The smoothness of them was delightful, and she lingered there. Soon she was moving a little, pushing her body up to meet her hand. She spread her fingers and slid them between her legs.

She was wet. A tiny moan escaped her.

She lifted her hand to her lips, licked first one finger, then another. She moaned again, a low and secret sound, something for herself alone. She tasted sweet, maybe even a little sweeter than usual. She suddenly remembered the toy in her hand. She slid it across her thigh and let out a shuddering breath. She wanted to be filled, to be slammed hard, to be made love to. All at once.

She pushed the toy against her clit. Her moan was louder this time, and the sensation rolled through her with the force of a fast-moving wave. Good grief—had she really been that tense? The relaxation and the tension combined together, made her struggle to move slow.

"Slow," she said out loud, taking a deep breath. The toy slipped against her clit, back and forth, warming even more as her wetness spread over it. She arched up and took the tip inside her. Her pussy was as smooth as her legs were. The wetness flowed unchecked across her lips and down the crack of her ass. She would have to change the sheets later. She didn't care.

Her mind slipped away to another place. There was a man hovering above her, a fantasy behind her closed eyelids. She didn't see his face, but she heard his voice in her head, the familiar, smooth tone that turned her on when he said those oh-so-right things.

You want that, don't you? You want my cock.

She wiggled her hips back and forth, trying to take in more of the toy. Her hand at the base of the toy was trembling. Her other hand was playing with her nipples, pinching them into hard little nubs, sending shocks of delight through her whole system.

She slipped the toy in another inch. The walls of her pussy stretched deliciously around it. She bit her lip as her boyfriend's voice whispered again in her head, and she imagined she could feel his strong arms on either side of her, holding his weight above her body. A drop of sweat rolled down her forehead, and she imagined that it had dripped from the man in her mind.

You like that, don't you? You can't get enough.

The word *slut* crossed her mind, and as it did, her man chuckled in her ear.

"Slut," huh? That's what you like to be called? Slut. You're a good one, aren't you?

She arched up and slid the toy home. It made her gasp, made her whimper, made her stretch. It made the man in her mind laugh out loud.

Look at you, how bad you need it. You're a slut, you're in heat, and you're ready to take on the whole neighborhood. Aren't you?

She was right on the edge. That fast, that hard, that steep was the climb. She withstood it for three long strokes, and with the fourth, she turned her head into the pillow to muffle the scream as she came.

Amber lay quietly, dazed. The orgasm had knocked the breath from her.

The whole neighborhood, he taunted again.

She reached blindly and found the toy box. Without opening her eyes, she felt around until she found what she wanted. What she needed. She grabbed it from the box and let it drop on the bed beside her. For now.

Oh, look at that. You really are a slut, aren't you? How many do you want?

She spread her legs wider. The toy still inside her began to move in and out of her again, harder this time, long strokes that made her want to moan. She got the angle just right, and the tip of the toy hit her G-spot, just like her boyfriend did, with every good thrust. Her heart pounded. She could come a dozen times like this, if only she had the patience.

Patience was never her strong suit.

She abandoned playing with her nipples and grabbed the second toy. It was longer than the other, but a bit thinner—perfect for what she had in mind. She was more than wet enough. She could feel it on the sheets underneath her.

You want to fuck more than one, don't you? You need it that bad, you naughty little slut.

Her mind was wiped clean of anything but the sensation. The pounding on her G-spot, the approaching orgasm, the feeling of pressure as she pushed the second toy against the hole that hadn't been touched in so very long. . . .

Do it. Do it right now.

She whimpered aloud as the toy pushed, stretched, breached. She caught her breath and bit her lip hard as it slid deep inside. She was completely full, and when the wave of orgasms hit her, she groaned aloud at the throbbing that seemed to claim every part of her.

That was a good one, said the man in her head.

But not good enough. She lifted a bit, moved in the right way, and then she was sliding the toy in and out of that little hole, impaling herself on it, moving in all the ways that made her body flush and tighten and beg. She imagined his warm breath against her ear, the deep thrusting, the male voice in companionship with hers.

You want me to come, don't you? You want to feel me fill you up.

"God, yes," she whispered aloud.

Both holes. Hot, sticky cream in both of them. That's what you want, isn't it?

The thought of it assaulted her, the warm and deep feeling, the spurt and run and flood that came along with the sound, the deep voice moaning in unison with her, the pulse of his body as he shot into her, over and over and over again—

She bit down on her lip, hard enough to taste blood. She saw stars behind her eyelids. In her mind, she heard the groan and the sound of her name whispered with a masculine plea. She arched up one more time, and then she was *there*, her heart racing, her blood pounding, and her breath escaping in a small scream.

She came hard enough to push the toy out of her pussy with the final pulses of her orgasm. The one in her ass was still moving sweetly with the motion of her hand, plunging deep and moving hard. As the last of her orgasm flowed away, the toy slipped out of her. She collapsed there on the bed, her eyes still closed, her head filled with the fantasy.

She drifted in a cocoon of pleasure. She had the idle thought that she might try for more later, but somehow, she knew this wouldn't be another sleepless night. Tomorrow night, perhaps. But not this one.

Other thoughts of her boyfriend crept into her mind. She wondered if he would have liked to be there, to help her play with those toys, to replace one of them with himself.

Amber fell into a deep, dreamless sleep, thinking of him as she drifted away. She knew one thing for certain: No matter what he was doing, he wasn't having *nearly* as much fun as he could have been having with her.

First Date

BY LOUISE HOOKER

"Do you like that?" Ginny asked as she slowly pulled the thin strap of the lacy, semisheer lingerie off her shoulder. She could hear the moan over her computer's speakers, and she fought to keep her face pouty—the way Mr. Black liked it. "Do you want the other one down?"

Mr. Black's breath was coming out heavy. Mr. Black was, of course, not this client's real name. That was an option, to give the girl a fake name. Not that it mattered. The company only accepted credit or debit cards, but that was only after the call girl took the information down via electronic means. But it made them feel safer, less perverted, if you called them by the fake name they gave.

Ginny smiled seductively as she stood before the computer screen, then tugged down the other strap. Mr. Black gasped. She moaned as she traced a crimson nail down her ample cleavage, pulling out a silken red handkerchief she kept there for certain clientele.

"Oops," she said, carefully dropping it on the floor in front of the desk where her computer sat. She smiled at the screen, which showed only the standard desktop background. Mr. Black was one of the few clients who kept his webcam off, preferring to see Ginny without her being able to see him. Most clients liked to be seen, liked to lock eyes with her while they did all the dirty little things they liked. But Mr. Black only liked to watch, not to be watched. This made him one of the most difficult clients to satisfy, as she literally had to play it by ear alone.

"Pick it up," he ordered, his voice deeper than usual.

Ginny slowly licked her tongue out across her lower, vermillion lip. She tried her best not to do any forward-bending while working. She did not like the way it made the extra fat on her body look—and she really had some to spare, as she was at least eleven sizes bigger than the "perfect" dress size.

She had never really liked the look of her body, since all her fat seemed to place itself squarely on her stomach. Sure, her legs, arms, and face were a little thick, and her breasts were an ample, natural, 40DD, but she never really worried about how they looked. Her stomach, on the other hand, poked out in such a way that, if she stood just right, she looked pregnant. Because of this, her high school years had been hell. And even though that was six years ago—precisely a four-year degree, plus two years—she had still not fully abandoned her insecurities about her size.

Ginny fought hard to keep her face sensual as the feeling of shame crept up in her. She lightly bit at her lip now, accomplishing both the nervous twitches growing in her and keeping Mr. Black interested all in the same moment. Then she put on a grin as she slowly moved into a squatting position—another movement that made her self-conscious, though it was better than falling forward. However, before she could even begin to reach for the handkerchief, Mr. Black cleared his throat.

"Not like that. Bend over. Let me see those tits."

There was no way around it. She straightened her body and nodded. She leaned way forward, exaggerating the movement, letting Mr. Black see exactly what he wanted. He gasped at the full-frontal view as she plucked the handkerchief from the floor.

"Stay like that, baby," he pleaded, an all too familiar sound of forced air escaping quickly. She also heard the sound of flesh meeting flesh, over and over and over again. It was almost a flapping noise, like something had come loose, and the usual moaning that always came with it let Ginny know she was doing exactly what she was being paid to do.

"Are you going to cum, baby?" she whispered directly into her computer's microphone.

"I'm so close."

She wiggled her shoulders, letting the lingerie fall completely off her upper half. With a few moans herself, she moved her hands over her exposed breasts. The noise coming from the computer intensified as Mr. Black gasped.

"Sit down. Let me see you finish."

Ginny blinked. This was not one of his normal requests. Usually, he did not give a rat's ass whether she had an orgasm or not. But that was okay; that was part of the job. The guys linked in and paid their ample sum so *they* could get off, not her. But she nodded, pulling up her desk chair and propping her left foot up on the seat. She let her knees fall wide and slipped her hand down her stomach—fighting the sense of awkwardness that welled up with that sensation—and reached inside her lace panties. Finding herself wet (it was inevitable, no matter how she felt about the man on the other side of the screen), she put her fingers to her clitoris, rubbing hard and fast there.

"Yes. Yes!" she groaned, squirming in place.

"Faster, faster."

She followed his orders, finally feeling her toes curl and seeing explosions of color in front of her closed green eyes. Mr. Black cried out, gasping with shuddering breaths, soon after.

"Was it good for you?" she asked.

"Yeah, baby. I'll be calling you again soon," he said.

She grinned. He always did. In fact, she would not be surprised to hear again from him tomorrow.

"I'll be waiting," she moaned, blowing the screen a kiss.

Ginny got no reply to that, and she did not need one. She knew Black had signed off, and she leaned over to close down her chat, too.

Standing and redressing herself in the lingerie—and with a robe to cover up now—Ginny made her way into the bathroom.

It took only a minute to do what she did after every meeting with a client. She ran a brush through her long, blond hair and reapplied the crimson lipstick she wore only for work. She glanced at the clock she kept on the bathroom wall. She still had an hour left before her self-appointed quitting time—ah, the joys of working from home.

Turning on her heel, she made her way back to her laptop and reopened the chat. She smiled at the name that instantly appeared under ONLINE. Her hand itched to click it, to open it, but that was taboo in her business. One of the first rules on the list her "boss" gave her was to always let the client come to you. So she waited a moment longer, and finally, the invitation to chat popped up. She clicked ACCEPT with a smile.

"Justin, baby, are you feeling hot this evening?" she chuckled.

Justin was another one of her regulars, but he was easily the strangest customer she kept—and the only one she would work overtime for. His honey-colored hair was a little on the shaggy side (a hairstyle she had suggested for him), and his brown eyes were as bright as his smile.

He shook his head. "I'm just talking tonight," he answered.

She nodded. "Just checking."

Her first meeting with Justin had happened a year ago—he was one of only ten of her regulars to have lasted so long. The first time, he had been just like any other customer: He paid his money, unzipped his pants, and told her what he wanted to see her do. His requests that first time had been typical: undress slowly; bounce her breasts a little, like she was riding him (another movement that made her feel like a jiggling fatty); and finger herself until they both came.

But when he called back two weeks later, he only wanted to talk.

Now, their meetings went back and forth between dirty little encounters and simple conversations. He easily knew more about her than any other client, and while that would make most of the other girls in the business a little uneasy, it made Ginny feel kind of nice.

"Talking it is, then. How was your day?" she asked, leaning back and tying shut her robe.

"Same old, same old. Work, home, and chatting with you, which is my favorite part of my day, by the way. Did you have many clients tonight?" he asked, his face and tone a little too even.

This was always a loaded question. Some nights, when Justin was feeling a bit frisky, the truthful "yes" that usually came in response to that question gave him instant wood. But other nights, it made him frown. Tonight, it would seem, was one of those other nights, and he looked a little bit more tense about it than usual.

She nodded.

"Oh," was his only response.

"It's my job, baby," she said, fidgeting in her seat.

She hated it when he looked disappointed or angry with her—something she didn't give a damn about when it came to the others. But Justin was a little bit more than just another client, another job, to her. It was trouble, and it made her feel horrible about charging him just to chat with her . . . but those were facts that were not easily changed.

"I've been thinking about some things," he said, when he finally got his teeth to unclench.

"Oh?"

"I want to meet you, for real. In person. Like, on a date."

Ginny blinked. This was bad. Really bad. Alarms began ringing almost instantly in her head—red flags going up all over the place. She shook her head. "I don't date clients, Justin, you know that. You've asked about the rules before."

"Is that an official rule, or a personal one?"

"Personal."

"Have you ever actually dated a client before?"

She shook her head.

"Then why not?"

Ginny laughed at that one. "Gee, let me think. Well, for one, it would be a little awkward."

"How so?"

"You've seen me finger myself, fuck myself with a toy and my finger, and lick my own tits, Justin. I think that's a bit more pressure than there usually is on a first date."

"I don't care about all that. I like you, for real. Let me take you out for dinner. You've mentioned before that we only live across the city from one another."

"So you want to buy the cow, when you've already had the milk?"

"You're not a cow."

His face was stony, serious. She frowned. He knew her better than any of her other clients. Hell, some of the other clients could not even remember her name. She was just the woman on the other end of the screen, doing dirty stuff for them for cash. But Justin had talked to her, had asked her about things—real, personal things. And he knew how she felt about her body. Never mind that it raked in cash in the thousands per week from people who liked to see a little meat on a girl's bones. She still had moments when she felt like an overstuffed . . . well, cow.

"You know what I meant," she whispered, unable to get her response out any higher.

"You're smart. You have a degree, for the love of God. You're funny. You're nice. And, to me, you're beautiful. All I'm asking for is dinner, maybe a movie. Is that so horrible? I mean, really. No strings attached."

"No. You're a client, Justin."

"I'm more than that."

"Honey, I'm still charging you by the minute here. No, you're not."

She regretted the words. They were much harsher than she had intended, but Justin just shrugged.

"I care about you. None of the others do."

"Whatever."

Ginny was almost constantly shaking her head now. This was all ludicrous. He was deluded, that was all. A girl did things for him, and all he had to do was ask. He definitely had that mixed up with "love" and "caring."

"I bet you that none of your other clients know about that one time, in high school, when those jocks filled your purse to the brim with tater tots and laughed at you, calling you names, when you opened it."

She pursed her lips. Ginny had no idea why she had told him what was probably her most horrible memory, and now that he was throwing it back at her, her body shook with rage and regret. Justin chuckled, continuing.

"And I bet that none of them know about how you used your first paycheck from that fast-food job to buy all the gay porn and personal lubricant you could, and then filled their backpacks with it for revenge."

She laughed, feeling her anger subside. That was one of her better memories. "You know, one of those jocks came out two years later," she said, and laughed again. Justin joined in.

"See? Do you do this with any other client? Honestly?"

"No," she admitted.

"Dinner. Tomorrow night. I know this Italian place that's

right between where we live. What have you got to lose?"

"A client."

"You'll lose me anyway if you say no."

"What?" Ginny said, leaning toward the screen. "Are you blackmailing me into dating you?"

"No, no!" he answered, waving his hands hurriedly. "I just mean . . . I *do* really care for you. I can't stop thinking about you. And it's hurting me to only see you like this. I want more, but if you won't give me that chance . . . I just can't go on hurting myself like this."

Ginny's heart thudded against her chest. He was going to stop it all? No more chats? Nothing? She had lost clients before, to simple things like steady girlfriends and marriage, but . . . "All right," she said. "What time do you want me to meet you there?"

Justin did nothing to hide his triumphant grin. "Seven, if that's alright?"

That was a prime time for her work. She was going to be out hundreds of dollars just by missing one night. She nodded anyway. "I'll be there."

⁂

From the start of their date, Justin had been nothing short of a gentleman from the start. When she arrived at the table, he stood and pulled out her chair. And when she ordered the salad, he scoffed and urged her to order what she wanted to eat, not what she thought she *should* eat. He complimented her appearance, saying that she looked good in the plum dress she had chosen for the evening. Despite the obvious change of atmosphere and clothing—and despite the involvement of food other than their usual sensual fruits and chocolate—it felt just like another one of their "conversation" nights.

And he was funny. Ginny could not remember the last time she had laughed so hard, or so frequently. By the end of dinner, her nose was still hurting from the water she had snorted out of it half an hour earlier.

"So," she said, trying to catch her breath while the waiter fetched the check, "you played chess in high school, *and* you were in the math club?"

He laughed, nodded. "Guilty as charged. I also had some hellish acne."

"I don't believe you." And she didn't. He was not muscular —no sculpted abs to be seen—but he was thin and seemed well built anyway, with his strong-looking, squared shoulders and shapely legs. Ginny had spent some of the night sucking her gut in, feeling a little exposed sitting with him. But he was kind to her, and he even dared to rest a hand on top of hers—and she felt no desire to pull hers away.

When he took her home that evening, she had not meant for anything to happen. When she invited him up, her sole intention was only to continue their pleasant conversation.

But they were only in her apartment ten minutes before they were in the bedroom, desperately clawing at each other's clothes.

"I don't do this, normally," she said as he made short work of her dress, letting it fall to the floor.

"I believe you," he moaned, pressing his mouth to hers as she pulled off his shirt and undid his jeans. His tongue made a tingling path up and down the left side of her neck as his fingers undid the clasp of her bra. He moved his hands down to the small of her back, gently laying her down on the bed. "Oh god, how I've wanted this," he moaned as he flicked his tongue down onto her right nipple.

Her back arched, and she reached for his swollen member. She gripped it tightly, jerking him as his mouth moved back to hers. He moaned, moving a hand down to her nether regions. He grinned at her.

"You're so wet."

He rubbed his thumb across her clit, which sent her legs into shaking. She clawed at his back, pushing her pelvis toward his groin.

"Please," she pleaded. "I want you in me."

He pulled himself free of her grip, and she groaned as he kissed his way down her stomach. His mouth hovered over warm parts, and she fought the urge to bolt right out of the bed.

"Don't," she said, leaning up.

He arched a brow at her. "Why not?"

"I'm not . . . I don't feel right when someone does that to me. I feel . . . I feel like it's just someone playing with my fat."

He chuckled, gently pushing her back against the pillows. "Then you've never had it done right."

And boy, was he right about that. As soon as his tongue connected with her, she felt a wave of pleasure wash over her. Her hands dug into the bed sheet, and her legs wrapped about his head involuntarily. She could feel him sucking at her now, and she longed to be doing the same to him. Finally, she exploded, feeling a new surge of wetness gush into his mouth. He moaned as he pulled himself over her.

"Let me do it," she begged. "Let me suck your dick."

"We'll save that for next time," he said, and Ginny felt his hard dick slide smoothly inside her.

She moaned and cried out with every thrust. She leaned upward into him, pressing her sweat-soaked breasts into his chest. It was not long before another orgasm rocked her body, followed shortly by his. Satisfied, the two collapsed next to one another.

It had been a long, long time since someone else had given her this kind of pleasure, and the sheer amount of it left her exhausted. Blinking sleepily, her eyes finally closed for the night.

⁘❧❧⁘

Ginny felt immediately stupid when she awoke in the morning. Justin was nowhere to be seen. She knew she should have known better. He had been a client after all, and her boss had warned her about the occasional client who would fake feelings just to get his for free.

But no one had warned her about how much it would hurt. She sniffled . . . and stopped. *Eggs. Bacon. Hash browns.* Ginny slowly raised up in bed, careful to hold the sheet against herself. She sniffed again and found the smells of breakfast unmistakable. She dove for her dresser drawer, pulling free the first T-shirt and pair of sweats she could find and putting them on. She made short work of the small hall between the bedroom and the kitchen and was greeted with a smile when she arrived.

Justin, dressed only in his jeans, was grinning at her,

gesturing to the round dining table where he had arranged two place settings. He walked over to the table.

"Hungry?" he asked, as he scooped scrambled eggs onto one of the plates.

Ginny nodded, sliding into a chair as he did the same for the other plate. The bacon and hash browns followed, and then he sat down with her.

"I had a great night," he said, lifting a fork.

Ginny blinked, unable to do anything but sit there. "Um. Me too."

He lifted a brow. "What's wrong?"

"I thought . . . I mean, you weren't there when I woke up."

"Did you think I just ditched you?"

She nodded, feeling her cheeks redden. Justin rolled his eyes. He reached across the table and took her hand in his.

"Now you listen to me, Ginny, and listen good. Sure, I met you as a call girl that caters to men who like bigger girls. And yeah, about half of our previous meetings had you doing just that, getting me off for a price. But I'm not the kind of guy to treat someone like that. And I meant what I said. I really care about you. And I would like to continue seeing you on a nonclient basis. Is that too much to ask?"

Ginny glanced down at herself. The T-shirt was way oversized—which meant it would be a tent on Justin—and the sweats she was wearing were stained with various foodstuffs. She was frowning deeply when she looked back at him.

"Are you sure you want this?" she said, gesturing to herself.

He rolled his eyes again. "Just shut up," he said, leaning across to kiss her.

When he went back to his food, Ginny grinned. She began to reach for her fork and stopped. Looking up, Justin arched a brow at her.

"What is it? Doesn't it look good?"

"It does, but . . ."

"Yeah?"

"Can I get a double helping of these hash browns?"

He laughed, standing and reaching for the pan. "Sure thing, baby."

At Last

BY JESSICA LENNOX

Nan and I have been friends for as long as I can remember—and for just as long, I've had an enormous crush on her. I don't know where I fit exactly in her head, but there is no mistaking the undeniable sexual tension between us. Even so, we have remained "just friends," despite all my flirting and innuendo.

I give Nan all the credit for keeping our friendship intact. If it were up to me, we'd have crossed that boundary long ago, but Nan is a serial monogamist and is currently involved with a Barbie-doll type named Megan. Apparently it doesn't make any difference to her that Megan lives five states away—the relationship is still worthy of "monogamy" status. I guess I should be happy about it, since doing the long-distance thing gives Nan plenty of free time to spend with me.

For more than ten years, Nan and I have spent hours, sometimes days, together, doing normal, everyday stuff—shopping, movies, lunch, dinner, whatever—and for just as many years, I have lusted after her. Aesthetically, I don't think we make a great couple—she's big and tall, and I'm short and round, with curves in all the right places. She's a good ten inches taller than me; I'm sure we look funny walking together side by side. But my lust for her trumps all that. I want to grab handfuls of her big body and pull her into me as I rub my body all over hers. She looks like she's built for hours of hard labor, and I'd love nothing more than to put her stamina to the test.

Alas, it remains a fantasy. Nan has set the boundaries firmly in place, and I try to respect that while I continuously torment myself with fantasy after fantasy.

I try to be content with what we have. In some respects, we've built a life together, and I take great comfort in that—in knowing she's there for me. I have a better relationship with Nan than I've ever had with anyone I've ever dated, but there are days when I feel such longing for her that I have to stop myself from begging her to break up with Megan and live her life with me. But eventually I talk myself down from the ledge and again resign myself to the fact that Nan and I *are* going to grow old together, as "just friends."

But last weekend things took quite a turn. It started out as just another Saturday. Nan and I were hopping around town. Spring was in full bloom, and everything looked happy and radiant. I was feeling particularly giddy, probably due to too much caffeine and sugar at breakfast. I made a point of touching her arm whenever I could, making plenty of sexual references, and flirting shamelessly with her. She kept looking at me out of the corner of her eye, and whenever she did, I made sure to play with my hair, or touch my lips, or caress my skin—anything to keep her attention on me.

As the minutes ticked on, I could feel the tension between us building. I paused momentarily to ponder why I was still torturing myself this way. I should have known by then that she wasn't ever going to give in. She'd said as much, hadn't she? And hadn't her iron will for the last ten years proven it?

I decided to give us both a reprieve and asked her about Megan.

"I don't know, she just seems so . . . I don't know," Nan answered.

"What do you mean? She just seems so what?"

"I don't know. I don't know," Nan said, showing frustration, her voice going up an octave.

Although I'd been flirting up a storm only moments before, my mood quickly shifted to "concerned friend." No matter how much I wanted to get naked with Nan, I considered her to be my dearest and truest friend, and if she was distressed, I wanted to know what was going on.

I tried coaxing her into talking more about Megan, but she just shook her head and said she didn't want to talk about it, so I eventually just left it alone.

The rest of the ride home was quiet, but finally we arrived back at her house and decided to make dinner and watch a movie. We cooked together, making small talk while moving around the small kitchen effortlessly.

I set the table while Nan put the finishing touches on our meal. We ate mostly in silence. Nan was brooding, and while I was tempted to lighten the mood, I wanted to let her feel whatever she was feeling. I wanted to ask more about Megan, but her mood made it pretty clear that Megan was an off-limits topic, at least for the time being.

When dinner was over, I cleared the dishes, and Nan grabbed a bottle of wine and two glasses, motioning for me to follow her into the living room. She poured the wine while I set up the movie to play. I got comfortable on the sofa as she settled into a chair across from me.

As the previews started, I sipped my wine and looked at her—studied her, really. She had flawless, smooth skin, and her short hair had a touch of salt and pepper. I wanted to run my hands through that hair. I let my gaze drift down her tattooed arms to her hands, which were strong and tan and made me wet just thinking about what they could do to me. By now, I'd forgotten all about the movie and instead continued to think about those hands on my body. I don't know how long I'd been indulging in my fantasy, but when my eyes traveled back up to her face, she was staring at me with a fierce intensity. All I could do was stare back at her. As I felt a hot flash radiate throughout my entire body, I broke into a smile and said, out of sheer nervousness, "What?" Then I swallowed hard.

She looked at me for another moment, then lowered herself to the floor and crawled the short distance that separated us. I raised one eyebrow, as if to silently ask what she was doing. She answered by placing her hands on my knees and slowly spreading my legs apart. As she moved her hands underneath my skirt and up my thighs, I was so surprised that I just sat there and let her. Not that I would want to protest anyway.

"Is this okay?" she asked, her voice quiet and unsure.

I wasn't sure what she was asking—or rather, in what context she was asking it—but I didn't think now was the time for a semantics debate, so I had to think for a moment, choosing my response. "I don't know. Is it?"

"I'm sick of overthinking it," she whispered, moving her hands farther upward until her fingertips were resting on the outside of my panties.

I had to admit, with her doing that, I wasn't thinking at all about whether or not it was okay. I just knew it felt good. I could feel the warmth of her fingertips through the fabric of my panties, and I swear it felt like my lips were purposefully engorging themselves with blood so that they could become fuller and therefore press up against her fingertips.

I spread my legs a little farther, dizzy with the realization that this was finally happening. I'd waited for it for so long, yearned for it, and finally, it was happening. Despite my joy, some part of me screamed *You shouldn't be doing this!* But the rest of me was saying a silent prayer of thanks as I let my eyes sweep over her broad shoulders, her muscular arms, her solidness.

I arched my hips a little and looked straight into Nan's eyes. As her fingers teased me, I had no doubt she could feel my wetness seeping through the fabric. All the attention to my pussy was making my nipples ache and stand at attention, and I found myself wishing she had more than two hands.

I reached forward and grabbed Nan's hair, tugging on it and pulling her toward me. As she leaned forward, she traced a line with her tongue from my neck down to my cleavage, then reached up with one hand to unbutton my blouse while the other continued to play with the edge of my panties. As I ran my fingernails down the back of her neck, she circled my nipples through my bra, then pulled on them, finally pulling my bra up and over my breasts so she could have full access to them.

She seemed to be moving in slow motion, and I couldn't help but think this was like slow torture. I'd wanted to fuck her for so long; I felt a sense of urgency, and everything seemed to be going in super-slow motion. She continued to tease my nipples and pussy, and when I thought I couldn't take it anymore, I felt her fingers slip underneath the fabric and into my swollen cunt. I moaned as I arched upward, running my fingernails down her back, encouraging her to continue.

"Is this okay?" she asked again, her words slightly muffled as she pressed her lips against my skin. I didn't answer but instead moaned loudly, pressing my pelvis forward, forcing her fingers to go deeper.

"I've wanted to fuck you for so long," she moaned. "You're so hot. God, you're so hot."

I leaned back against the chair and arched my hips upward. "Fuck me harder . . . harder," I gasped.

Nan groaned, a sound that made me shiver as I felt her push another finger into my pussy. I felt her other hand slide down, her fingers moving into the grooves on each side of my clit, trapping it, tugging on it. A few more strokes and I felt that twinge—the one that signals the beginning of my orgasm. It wouldn't be long now, and no matter what I thought about, I wouldn't be able to distract myself from the explosion that was moments away.

"I'm gonna come on your hand," I gasped, clamping my muscles around her fingers. "Oh fuck, yeah," I groaned, squeezing my legs together and digging my fingernails into her skin. "Don't stop . . . please don't stop," I begged.

"That's it," she said, coaxing me, "come for me." I felt another wave building and reached down to still her hand. I didn't need any more movement, I just wanted to ride and rub up against her at my own pace. She kept her hand there, letting me rock on it, and moved the other to unbutton her jeans, reaching inside and rubbing herself furiously. I could see the muscles on her arms bulging and a sheen of sweat on her forehead.

She looked fucking hot, and I thought I might come again, just from watching her get off. Finally she gritted her teeth and groaned, leaning forward and burying her face in my breasts. I dug my fingers into her shoulders and came with her, one of my hands tugging on her hair as my cunt pulsed around her fingers. Then we both collapsed.

As we lay there panting, the annoying voice in the back of my head began asking questions. *Now what? Would she tell Megan? Would this ruin our friendship?*

I was so deep in thought that I jumped when Nan suddenly asked, "Are you okay?" She lifted herself into a sitting position to look at me.

I paused, trying to come up with an accurate answer. "I don't know. I'm confused, I think. More important, are *you* okay?"

Nan smiled, taking my hands in hers. "I'm more than okay. I don't think what we did is wrong. I love you. How can it be wrong?"

I smiled, more confused than ever, but frankly, I wasn't in the mood to debate. I just wanted to enjoy this moment, for however long it would last.

Wenching

BY JUSTINE ELYOT

Lady Bray berated me through the castle kitchen and toward the changing room. "These medieval banquets are good for business. If we want to keep the gift shop and your job open, we need to book a few more. The weddings alone aren't bringing in enough revenue. So I'm sure you're going to take off that sulky face and put on a nice big smile for our clients, aren't you?"

My response was halfway between a grunt and a sigh. I knew she was speaking sense, but I was distracted by the divine scents of roasting meat and spices. The usually frigid basement was warm, and it was filled with the clattering of pans and the chopping of vegetables.

"I didn't realize the ovens still worked," I told her, watching, with fascination, as coal was shoveled into the vast black range.

"Spent a fortune getting them ready," she sniffed, then turned to a kitchen hand. "Good gracious, woman, haven't you ever plucked a guinea fowl before?"

"Well . . . no," she admitted, tugging dubiously at brown feathers.

❧❦❧

The room beyond the kitchen—formerly, it was the scullery—was where I was to be transformed from twenty-first century gift-shop assistant to thirteenth-century peasant wench. I had been dreading it for weeks.

It was fine for Beth and Joanna, with their teeny waists and barely there bosoms, but the costume hanging on the rail for me was embarrassingly labeled XL.

"The skirt's got an elasticized waist," said Beth, trying to help. She was already laced into her kirtle, or whatever those things were called. "So at least it's comfortable."

"Yeah, stylish," I drawled, holding up the hanger bearing my kirtle. A dreary cascade of patched brown fabric depressed my eye.

I slouched behind the curtain and began to take off my tunic and leggings. I might be a big girl, but at least I know what looks good on me—and elasticized, floor-length skirts most definitely don't. I could hear Beth and Joanna whispering on the other side of the divide, and—although they were okay, really—I briefly entertained hatred for them and their pert asses and their willowy hips. It wasn't their fault that we had to do this, but I foresaw a long evening of humiliation and irritation ahead, and they just happened to be available as targets of my silent angst.

The skirt, as predicted, was foul, and it looked even worse when I teamed it with the white peasant blouse with a low, gathered neck. The bloody thing was off the shoulder, so I had to take off my bra and let my tits just flop there. The flyblown mirror in front of me must have had to muster all its strength not to crack, there and then.

"D'you want me to lace your stays, Gin?" called Joanna, and it was only then that I realized there was a third element to the costume: a black velvet corset-type thing that laced up the front.

"Just a mo." I placed the stay around what other people call their waist—it just about fit—and pulled the laces. "Yeah, could you?"

Joanna got hold of each string and pulled so hard I began to cough. But when she had laced them up and stepped back, she whistled admiringly. "Christ, Ginny, you have cleavage to die for. Look in the mirror."

I didn't want to, but she forced me, with a hand on my shoulder. And I must admit, my reflection made me blink, then put my hands on my hips and shimmy. Shimmying is not something I do often, but I was so taken aback by this illusion of a figure that the waist cincher had given me, I just couldn't resist the urge.

"Beth, come and check out the hourglass! She's like Marilyn Monroe."

"Yeah, a ginger Marilyn Monroe who ate too many pies," I snarked, but my cheeks were pink with the secret thrill of looking not bad for once.

"You look lush," said Beth. "And I've always said I'd kill for skin like yours."

Yeah, yeah, the "perfect skin" comment—always made as implicit compensation for the unmentionable flab. I am always the elephant in the corner. But with better skin.

"Those medieval blokes are going to spill their ale when they get a load of you," said Joanna.

"Or vomit up their guinea fowl," I said, pathologically self-deprecating as ever.

"Oh, shut up. Get out there and strut your stuff, wench."

∞⚬§⚬∞

The jugs of spiced wine were heavy, so my attempts at a slow, sexy sashay probably turned out a little lopsided, and it's hard to shake your booty without spilling drops on the floor.

The long banqueting table was filled with people who had replicated medieval dress with varying degrees of success. They were diving into the punch and mead with a will, already plum-cheeked and rowdy, talking and laughing over the lute player in the gallery. The jester was doing his best but was largely ignored, though the roasted guinea fowl seemed to be a hit.

It was second nature to me to shrink back into the shadows, so I found an unobtrusive spot and left most of the refilling to Beth and Joanna, who seemed popular as always with the male contingent.

I was lurking close to the fire, warming myself in its flickering flame, enjoying the music, when I noticed I was being watched.

He was reclining, with his arm on the back of his chair—a dark-haired man with a plate of bones in front of him. He was handsome—the kind of man I'd worship from afar but never dream of approaching. I supposed he was in some kind of reverie, not realizing that I was even there, but when I moved a little farther to the left, away from the fire, his eyes followed me.

I swallowed and hugged the jug closer to me. *Why would he be looking at me? Why would* anybody *want to look at me?* I avoided his penetrating gaze, staring down at the mulled wine, whose sweet, potent steam drifted up to bead my face with moisture.

When I looked up again, he raised a hand in a beckoning gesture. My chest constricted, and I had to try hard not to cackle hysterically.

"Me?" I mouthed.

His perfectly curved lips rounded to an O. "You," he mouthed back, then tossed his head in further summons.

I nearly dropped my jug, but I managed to keep a tenuous grip on it and stepped out of the shadows, into the orbit of the tipsy revelers.

"Nice jugs—I mean, jug!" leered one charmer, to general mirth, and I was back to earth with a bump. *Thanks for the timely reminder.* Big Ginny, the big butt of big jokes.

I lost my nerve and moved back into the shadows. I didn't look at the beckoning man, but instead kept my eyes on the door that led out to the battlement. I was going to go out and have a cigarette and a few tears. Then I would come back and be the same useless fat biffer I was before I put this stupid costume on. It was ridiculous of me to forget for that one moment that I was entirely unattractive. Ridiculous!

I plonked the jug by the fireplace and fled.

Outside, the late summer sun was setting, and I leant over the wall between two crenellations and watched it, looking over the hills and valleys. I had stood in this spot many times, pretending to be a princess or a lady of quality from centuries past. My imagination was a good place to be. Perhaps I should go back there. For good.

When the door opened behind me, I assumed it was Beth or Joanna or, worse, Lady Bray come to give me a pep talk. I reached in my apron pocket for the cigarettes of defiance, but before I could locate them, a voice spoke—and it was a male voice.

"That man's a wanker," he said.

I whirled around, hugging my arms to my chest. The beckoner. He took a step forward and spoke again.

"Or perhaps I should say he's a jackanapes, or a poltroon, or something like that. If I'm going to stay in role."

I laughed. The man came closer. Dangerously close.

"It's okay. I'm used to comments like that," I said. Looking down at my breasts, I noticed that they were heaving. I wondered if the man was going to rip my bodice. Why would a man like this want to rip *my* bodice?

"Well, that's wrong. You shouldn't have to put up with it." He stood beside me, leaning back against the battlement, his arm nudging mine.

"That's life. If I don't like it, I suppose I'll just have to eat lettuce for a year."

"Oh no, you mustn't do that." His arm pressed closer. His chin butted my hair.

"Why not? I've had enough of it all. The looks of disgust on everyone's faces, the judgment, the assumptions that get made about me because I'm carrying extra tonnage and poundage. It makes me lazy, apparently, and slovenly and dirty and slack-jawed and stupid and . . ."

I broke off. I was stupid all right. I was also crying.

He slid an arm around me and hugged me into that hard, tight wall of muscle.

"We should be able to time travel," he said. "Back to an age when society was kinder to the Rubenesque woman."

"Hmph." I wasn't able to say much.

"I'd love that. I love softness. Love curves. The more, the better."

"D'you really?"

"Why wouldn't I? Think of all the words associated with a bit of extra flesh. Generous. Ample. Voluptuous. Bountiful. Beautiful, sensual words. Contrast them with their opposites. Mean. Insufficient. Meager. Miserly."

I snuffled into his velvet jerkin or doublet or whatever it was and looked up at him. "You should be a professional morale booster," I told him. "You're very kind to say all this but—"

"Kind?" he burst out. "No, I'm not kind! I don't feel sorry for you. I want you."

"You what?"

"When I beckoned you over, I didn't want a refill of that bloody horrible wine. I wanted to get you on my lap."

"Why?"

"Why d'you think, goose girl? Because I think you're gorgeous. What's your name?"

"Ginny."

"Richard. And I'll repeat, I think you're gorgeous, Ginny."

"No, Beth and Joanna—the other waitresses—are gorgeous."

"They're conventionally attractive. But they make terrible wenches. No rounded pillows of flesh spilling over the tops of their corsets. No curvaceous hips swaying under the skirts. Very poor effort. One out of ten. But you—you are a serious *wench*."

"I've missed my vocation."

"Yes, you have. I think you should always dress like this. Except when you're in bed. My bed."

"You're very bloody bold, aren't you?"

His answer to that was textbook. Hand in hair, soft lips turning hard, hot breath, plunging tongue—the most emphatic "yes" imaginable.

"As soon as I saw you," he crooned into my disarranged hair, "I wanted to touch you. I wanted to get my hands on those hips and bury myself in that feast of flesh. You feel even better than I thought you would. I'm not sure I'm going to be able to let go of you."

"I keep thinking you must be joking." My head was exploding. It was all too confusing. People were not supposed to fancy me.

"You need one thing, Ginny, just *one* thing, and then you'll be perfect."

"What's that?"

"Confidence. You'd be sexy as hell if you'd just stop trying to fold yourself up and make yourself invisible."

"I wish I could believe you. . . ."

"Do it! Believe me! Or you'll have me to answer to."

Our mouths, our hands, couldn't stay apart, and we fell back together on the battlement, kissing fulsomely against the sunset backdrop until the door opened again and Beth hissed, "Lady Bray is looking for you! Oh! Sorry. But she is."

"Shit, I should go!"

"Hie thee thither, fair lady," said Richard, propelling me forward with a light slap to my backside. "But when thou finishest thy task, I shall bear thee away with me. To the Feathers."

"You're staying at the Feathers?"

"Yeah, do you know it?"

"I work there most evenings."

"Of course you do. You're a wench. Come on then. Let's finish this feast so we can move on to a more adult version."

I was able to fob Lady Bray off with some story about needing fresh air. The medieval revelers were no less objectionable for the rest of the evening, but I didn't care. I was beyond their dull barbs. It didn't matter any more. I was desired by the best-looking man in the place.

"Do you know him?" muttered Beth on her way past. "He's *lovely*."

"Isn't he?" I said smugly. I would have said more, but Richard had reached out an arm as I passed and had bundled me onto his knee, holding me there while he joined in some kind of end-of-evening wassail with his friends, clashing tankards and drinking to the King—King Henry IV.

"I ought to get changed," I whispered, slipping off his lap as the plates were cleared and the guests rose to leave.

"No. Keep it on."

"It's not mine!"

"They won't miss it. Take it back tomorrow."

"I can't . . ."

"Then I'm going to have to have you here. Before you get changed."

"We can't . . ."

"You must know somewhere."

"Richard!"

"Ah, you do."

His voice was low, pouring into my ear while his hand lingered, hidden by his shadowing body, on my bottom.

I felt drunk with lust, all the spices tingling inside me, the wine of desire in my veins. I did know somewhere. I led him through a side door and up a staircase, past hanging flags and tapestries, until we were in a display bedroom, kept in Middle Ages style, with a four-post bed and ornately carved wooden chests.

Richard laughed, helped me over the red rope designed to keep visitors off the furniture, and pushed me down on the bed.

I had no qualms about this, knowing that none of the exhibits were genuinely old—they were all replicas. There were ordinary springs rather than rushes in the medieval mattress, and they creaked rustily beneath my weight. They positively groaned once Richard's tall, solid frame joined me, straddling me and pinioning me at the wrists before he swooped down to rub his stubbled face in my breasts, growling and nipping ravenously.

With his teeth, he pulled the gathered elastic of the peasant blouse down over my braless tits, setting them free. He took a big handful of each and squeezed, sighing with joy, before bending to suck at each nipple with his eager mouth.

"These should be painted," he said. "Or sculpted. I'd do it myself if I had an artistic bone in my body."

The most significant bone in his body had just now dug into my thigh through my frowsy brown skirt. I arched my spine and jiggled my pelvis beneath his, reminding him that I was more than a pair of breasts.

He had me roll over and kneel up while he removed the hated skirt, uncovering my bottom and thighs—to my cringing dread. But I need not have worried. He smacked the seat of my big cotton knickers and tutted at me.

"Wenches don't wear knickers. We'd better do something about that."

One hand still worked on my tits, kneading and pressing them, while the other wrenched down the knickers, bringing to light the dimpled flesh beneath.

"So much lushness," he whispered reverently, letting his palm glide over both my buttocks, then down the crack, reaching between my thighs and slapping their tender inner flesh gently, so that it wobbled. He pushed me down, so that my face fell against the rather rough bedcover, and proceeded to kiss my bottom all over, from the rounded cheeks and inward, to the dark furrow that bisected them. His tongue lapped at the sensitive hidden skin, and I began to twitch, my pussy convulsing, wanting him there, too, and yet still at my ass, and everywhere, all over my body, with simultaneous devilry.

Suddenly, his hands gripped my hips again, and he had me flat on my back, naked but for the black velvet bodice, legs spread and ready to envelop him in their ample warmth.

"I want to devour you," he said. His stubble scratched its way up the insides of my thighs, striking sparks on the journey, ending at my parted, soaked lips, and drinking them in, a reward well earned.

I writhed against his tongue, wanting to bathe it in endless nectar, wanting to draw him up inside me. The ceiling fittings blurred and danced around the corners of my eyes, while everything else, from neck to toes, melted into one hot mess.

The tip of his tongue flicked my clit from side to side until I came the first time, crying out in wonderment, unleashed at last from the tummy-concealing, boob-enhancing, bottom-controlling day-to-day reality that had kept me hidden and trussed up, away from the simple freedoms of life.

"Ginny, Ginny, Ginny, you should see your face," he told me, kneeling up between my thighs, grinning wicked white teeth down at me. "All that doubt and fear and confusion was gone. You looked like an erotic fucking goddess. Just as you should be."

"A goddess, *mmm.*" I stretched my arms out above my head, enjoying the way my breasts lifted. "That must make you a god."

"*Hmm,* well, if the cap fits . . ." He kissed a ring around my navel, laying his cheek against the ripples of my stomach for a moment.

He flipped me over again, placing the hard stuffed pillows under my hips, laying his own body over mine until our cheeks were side by side and his cock lay at the crease of thigh and perineum, ready to seat itself.

There was a pause for the application of the nonmedieval prophylactic, then a sweet, deep hiss of pleasure from us both as hard flesh met soft. My cunt was hungrier than my mouth, sucking him in, squeezing him tight, pushing back to beg an ever-firmer thrust, accompanied by the delicious slap of his pelvis against my broad bum cheeks.

Never had my weight felt better employed than in giving him extra handfuls to grab and slap and stroke. He certainly seemed to make the most of it, his hands and arms making contact with as much of my swaying surface area as they could, stilling my swinging breasts, pressing into my juddering thighs, finding the one small tight part of me with his cock and seating himself over and over again.

"Take thy master's yard in thy heated quaint, wench," he said, causing me to crane my neck around and query this odd statement.

"Yard? Quaint?"

My question gave me the opportunity to look at his glorious face, which had transformed—as a result of fierce concentration on the job at hand—from languid handsomeness to wicked beastliness.

His brow cleared for a moment. "Not a medievalist, Ginny? Ah well, I can educate you. *Hmm.* Now get on your back, wench. I want to see your face when you reach the moment of death. And I don't mean literal death. It's a euphemism for orgasm."

"Wow," I breathed, letting him flip me over and spread my thighs. "I've heard of getting medieval on someone's ass, but this—"

"Cheeky wench," he growled, and then he was back in, his lean lusciousness above me, his lips brushing mine. "I'll brook not thine impertinence."

"Okay, okay," I laughed, distracted by the archaic language and wanting to get back to the twenty-first-century shag. "Just give me what you've got, milord. Or . . . render me . . . what thou . . . hast. Or whatever."

He rendered me what he hadst in fine style, bringing us

both to a steaming, boiling, sticky climax that tipped us both over the brink.

For me, it was my biggest and best (admittedly of a poor field), but even as the rush of ecstasy dissolved, I found myself falling back into my habitual thought patterns, sure that this was just an opportunistic fuck for my beautiful medievalist.

I was already resigning myself for a brief vote of thanks and a "See you around" before the shamefaced sneak-out. Determined to preempt it, I sat up briskly and reached for my discarded head-scarf. "We'd better get going before Lady Bray finds us and I lose my job. That was nice. Thanks."

He propped himself up, screwing his eyes beneath his gorgeously disheveled brow. "Are you giving me the brush off? Oh god. You have a boyfriend. Of course you do. A girl like you . . ."

"God, no! I'm single. You think I'm some kind of slut?"

"I know you are," he said, winking. "The best kind."

I melted. I couldn't keep up this no-nonsense, don't-care front. "So . . . ?"

"So stop being so ridiculous and come back to my hotel with me. That was just a taster, my dear. I have plans for you."

"Plans?"

"For acts far beyond the medieval scope." He rebuttoned and tidied himself before extending a hand. I took it and followed him out of the bedroom and down the stone stairs, senses on high alert for signs of Lady Bray.

"Did you know, Ginny, that the medieval church frowned upon all sexual contact that wasn't strictly missionary?"

"No."

"Oh, yes. All sex had to be strictly for the purposes of procreation. And only on certain days of the year, too. That's one of the things that makes me glad to be alive now." We slunk through the kitchens—past the washers-up and the oblivious porters—to the scullery. "The only thing that really bugs me about modern times," he sighed, "is the terrible shortage of wenches. But I think I've solved that problem now."

"Yeah." I laid my head on his shoulder as his arm wrapped tight around me. "Let's hope so."

What Girls Are Made Of

BY EVAN MORA

There's this saying, maybe you know it, about what makes girls girls (sugar and spice and everything nice) and what makes boys boys (snips and snails and puppydog tails).

I would tell you that I think the "girl" part is absolutely true, because I'm most definitely sweet like sugar, and I can give you a rush that's better than a whole Halloween pillowcase full of candy —and that, let me tell you, is *everything* nice. And spice? Hell, I've got that in abundance.

I love spice. It's what fires people up, what makes them get all hot under the collar. It's what makes a girl like me stand up and say *I don't care how fine the packaging is, snips and snails just ain't gonna do it for me. Not when there's so much sugar and spice out there.*

As it turns out, these ingredients—sugar, spice, everything nice—can combine all kinds of wonderful ways. There are girls of every shape, size, and color imaginable, each with her own personal blend of sugar and spice.

I'm happy to say that I've sampled my fair share of the flavors out there. But my very favorite combo—the peanut butter and chocolate of them all—is a dapper butch woman with a little substance to her. *Mmm-hmm.* And I say this with no disrespect to all the lean-hipped, washboard-fit butches out there. You are certainly yummy in your own right. But give me a handsome woman tucked into a pair of 36-by-30s, and I start to melt in all the right places.

If I'm on the dance floor and I spy that fly butch woman moving to the beat, I'm going to make my way over there and dance alongside her; see what I can do to catch her eye. I've got moves of my own, and I'm certainly not shy, and if she's appreciating me, and she sees that I'm appreciating her, then I'm going to move in a little closer and put my hand on her arm, give her a little smile, and say hi.

We're going to start to sway together, she and I, and this is one of my very favorite things, because even though there's a conversation made of small talk going on, there's another one going on between hands and bodies, all at the same time. I'm going to run my hand up her arm, over her biceps and broad shoulder and 'round to stroke the short soft hair at the back of her neck. She's going to wrap a strong arm around my waist, bring me in nice and close, and press a solid thigh between mine.

Now, I mentioned I've got spice in abundance—I'm feisty, some might say. And I'm no dainty, delicate femme either; I can hold my own in just about any situation. And this woman I'm dancing with? She already knows I'm bold enough to make my way over here and make my intentions clear. And what she's doing with that strong arm around my waist and solid thigh between mine? She's letting me know that she can handle my shit. And there is nothing sexier than a big, capable woman who knows she's got it going on.

She's going to give me a sexy, knowing smile then, before leaning in and kissing me breathless, making me curl my toes inside my kitten heels. She's going to slide her hand a little lower, cup my ass, and pull me a little tighter against her so I can feel the crush of her breasts beneath that freshly pressed shirt and the undeniable ridge of something strapped beneath those jeans. She's going to whisper in my ear, ask me if I want to go someplace, and I'll say yes, I know a place, and take her home.

I'm going to close my door, and she's going to press me up against it, lift me up and settle my legs around her waist, my skirt bunched around my hips, those big strong hands gripping the undersides of my thighs. We're going to move like that, tongues twining, hips rocking, breast to breast through all these layers of clothes. And when that's not enough, when we're all hot and bothered and those layers of clothes are too much to bear, I'll whisper, "Follow me," and lead her into my bedroom.

I'll let her undress me, like a good butch should, and she'll do it slow enough to let me know she's enjoying every minute of it. She'll have skilled hands, this woman, and a mouth that's pure sin, and she's going to put them to work, working me over until I need to come so bad I can't hardly think, and the only words coming out of my mouth are "Please, baby . . . ."

She'll laugh then—a wicked, sexy sound that'll go right to my pussy—and she'll pick me up like I weigh nothing at all and drop me down, right in the center of my queen-size bed. She'll kneel between my wide open legs, stroking that impressive looking bulge still tucked inside her jeans, and ask me if I'm ready for her. I'll say "Yes, baby," but she'll shake her head. "I don't think so," she'll say.

She'll cover my body with hers then, pressing me down into the bed while she settles her weight onto her forearms and sets to work with that mouth again, teasing a trail from my earlobe down the sensitive skin of my neck, making me shiver before she captures my mouth with hers and tangles her tongue with mine. All the while, she'll be rocking her hips up slowly against me, teasing me with the promise of that big fat cock I know she's got, the scrape of denim against my swollen clit driving me wild with need.

I'm going to be pulling at the hem of her shirt, trying to get at her skin, but she'll just capture my hands and pin them over my head, both my wrists held captive in one strong hand, and it won't matter how much I struggle, she isn't going to budge one bit. It turns me on, how strong and capable she is, how she holds me there without effort.

She'll get back to business, mouth on my skin, licking and sucking and biting a wet trail down my body until I'm moaning and pleading and I'm so ready for her that I'm soaking through the front of that finely pressed shirt of hers and the smell of my sex is all around us.

She'll let go of my wrists then, smooth that hand down the curve of my body and down between my thighs. She'll tease my wetness with her blunt fingertips and then push two thick fingers inside. She'll fuck me like that, curling her fingers a little, so that she's hitting my spot just right. And each time she thrusts, the pad of her thumb will stroke against my clit until I'm just about out of my mind. "Oh yeah," she'll say, "you're ready for me now," and then she'll suck my juices from her fingers. She'll kiss me once more so I can taste myself on her, and then she'll move off the bed so she can undress.

She'll slide each button through its hole, nice and slow, knowing she's got an appreciative audience, and when they're all undone, she'll shrug her shirt off, and her sports bra will follow close behind. She's got big, beautiful breasts and a slightly tucked-in waist, and I love the juxtaposition of her feminine curves with the low-slung men's jeans and the big silver buckle. She's sugar and spice—but something else, too, and I love how it all blends together. She's going to open that buckle, make slow work of the fly, while I bite my lip in anticipation. Then she'll reach inside, pull out that fat cock, and stroke it in her hand. "You like what you see?" she's going to say to me then, and I'll tell her that I do.

I'm going to do more than that though. I'm going to *show* her just how much I like it. I'm going to climb off the bed and press myself up against her, slip my tongue into her mouth. I'm going to kiss her until she groans, until those big strong arms close around me. And here's another thing I love—another seeming contradiction that makes me all weak in the knees—I love how *soft* she feels. She's rock solid and strong and proud of it, you can tell, but she's also deliciously soft and warm. I love the crush of her breasts against mine; the rounded curve of her belly pressed against me.

I'm going to kiss my way down the side of her neck, cup those big breasts with my hands. I'm going to tease her nipples until they're nice and tight and then pull each one into my mouth. I know some girls like their butches looking a little more boyish, a little more androgynously *flat*. But not me: I like breasts that fill up my hands, and a woman who appreciates their sensitivity. I'm going to take my time and really love those breasts until I hear her making little sounds of pleasure.

And when I hear those sounds, I'm going to let my hands trail lower, slip beneath the waistband of those open jeans. I'm going to help them slide down, past the curve of her hips; I'll kneel down and help her kick them off. I'm going to run my hands over her rounded calves and across the front of her wide, muscled thighs. Then I'm going to wrap my hand around that thick silicone dick and take it deep into my mouth. She'll widen her stance, cup the back of my head, rock her hips forward just a little. "That's it," she'll whisper, and I'll work it a little faster, because I know the base of that dick is hitting her clit just right.

It won't be very long, though, before she pulls me up and splays me wide on the edge of my bed. Then she'll thrust into me, hard and deep, and I'll wrap my legs around her hips, pull her in even tighter. I love the feel of all that strength pounding into me. Maybe later on we'll do it again, nice and slow, but for now, I want it fast and rough; I want sweat and fierce hungry kisses; I want to grab handfuls of her and sink my nails deep into her skin and come with a loud wailing cry all over her big fat cock.

And maybe she'll come, too, fucking me like that, and we'll collapse in a tangled sweaty heap. Or maybe she'll want to switch it up a little—want to lie on her back while I straddle those hips, sink down onto her cock, and grind my pussy against her until she explodes with a great heaving orgasm of her own. Maybe she'll even unbuckle her harness and come on my fingers and tongue. You never know. Sugar and spice, right?

At some point, she'll pick those 36-by-30s up off the floor and try to shake the wrinkles out of her shirt. She'll put it all back together and tuck it in just right. She'll check her reflection in the mirror above my dresser and will probably catch me checking out her ass. She'll give me a wink, flash a cocky smile, and I'll start to melt all over again.

Because a big butch woman who knows she's got it going on? Gets me every time.

Appetite

BY ELIZABETH COLDWELL

My basket is heaving with goodies. I've made a slow circuit of the supermarket—which is beautifully quiet in this midmorning lull before the lunchtime shoppers descend—picking out everything I need. I have thick, yellow Cornish clotted cream, a jar of rich Belgian chocolate dipping sauce, and a tub of ready-made custard infused with the finest Madagascan vanilla seeds. My mouth is almost watering just looking at it all.

The woman in line at the next checkout keeps glancing at the contents of my basket, then back to me, trying her best to be surreptitious in her movements, as though I won't realize what she's doing. I know exactly what she's thinking. She's made a mental note of all the rich, sweet, calorie-laden treats I'm buying, then attributed them to the heft of my hips and ass, the swell of my belly, the extra weight around my chin and the tops of my arms.

Because I'm fat, and because I'm buying all these things that seem designed purely to make me fatter, she's deduced that I'm greedy and lazy and stupid; that I don't take any care of my appearance; and that I am deserving of her contempt. By extension, she probably reckons I'm not getting any sex either.

On all these counts, she would be wrong.

While it's true the black vest top and knee-length shorts I'm wearing aren't exactly the most flattering items for a woman of my build, it's an unseasonably hot day, and I don't see the point in dressing up purely for a quick trip to the supermarket. And they'll serve me perfectly well for putting in a few miles on the exercise bike in our basement when I get home.

There's no denying it: I'm a big girl, and I have a big appetite. I love my food, and I always have. I'm not ashamed of that, and the pursed lips and disapproving glances of some self-righteous stranger in a checkout line aren't going to change my attitude. She can think what she likes. She probably didn't even notice all the fruit that's also in my basket: the ripe, juicy peaches; the succulent strawberries, fresh from the fields of Kent. Or maybe she did, and she simply chose to ignore them so as not to prejudice her impression of me.

When she looks over at me again, I catch her eye and smile. She turns away and pretends to be incredibly interested in a leaflet outlining the supermarket's ethical shopping policies. Move along, dear, nothing to see here. . . .

Still, I'd love to see the expression on her face if she knew what I'm intending to do with all this food.

When I get home, Matt has just returned from training and is making himself a mug of tea. His hair's still slightly damp from the shower, and he smells of the patchouli-scented soap he always uses.

He puts an arm round me, and we share a kiss. Pulling away, he asks, "Did you get everything?"

"Yeah. I'm just going to put it all away; then I'm off to work out for a while."

"Let me give you a hand with it."

That's what I love about Matt. Anything to make my life a little easier. As he bends to stow the cream on the lowest shelf inside the fridge door, I take a sneaky peek at his ass, which is outlined in his close-fitting tracksuit bottoms. I never tire of admiring his big, muscular body, the thighs that seem hewn from the sandstone of his native Rhondda Valley. Like most professional rugby players, he is classified as "obese" by the body mass index. Yet there's barely an ounce of fat on his six-foot-two frame. He's solid and powerful and in his deliciously masculine prime, and if I stand looking at him any longer, I'll be very tempted to drag him off to bed this minute, too impatient to wait for what we've planned this evening.

Matt turns round and catches me staring. "Hey, Eva, that fruit's not going to put itself in the bowl, you know."

The grin that suggests he knows exactly where my gaze has been fixed does nothing to damp down my rising desire. His appetite is as hearty as my own, and it will only take a word from me, but somehow, we both manage to control ourselves.

Between us, we finish stowing the groceries, and then I turn to leave the kitchen. As I do, Matt picks out one of the strawberries, biting down on it slowly with his small, white teeth. If I give him the opportunity, he'll tease me like this for the rest of the day, getting me so hot and bothered I can barely think straight. I head for the basement, for what I know will be a vain attempt to pedal away some of my frustration.

✦

The afternoon passes in sticky, feverish anticipation. Matt lounges on the couch in his T-shirt and boxers, playing some mindless shoot-'em-up adventure on his game console. I'm supposed to be reading through manuscripts, but the slush pile can be unrewarding enough at the best of times, and today it's just too hard to concentrate. Eventually I give up and go to get ready.

I take a quick shower, then shave my legs, armpits, and all but a tiny tuft of hair from my pussy, making sure my lips are lickably smooth. Swathed in my toweling dressing gown, I sit at the dressing table and apply makeup. Normally, I don't bother with much more than a slick of lip gloss and a little mascara, but now I outline my eyes with smoky kohl and brush the lids with dramatic shades of purple and gold. Blusher contours my cheeks, and matte plum lipstick completes the look. My reflection stares back at me, familiar but deliciously exotic. Just the effect I'd hoped for.

Matt's going to love this outfit, I think, looking at where I've laid it out on the bed. He told me to pick out something cheap and nasty, and this symphony of artificial fibers—found at the kind of market stall that sells fluorescent-pink fishnets and three-for-a-pound packs of thongs—really fits the bill. It's a black babydoll nightdress so sheer that the dark, puckered points of my nipples are clearly visible through it. The matching split-crotch panties are so scratchy and uncomfortable, I'd never be able to wear them for any serious length of time. Hopefully, I won't have them on for very long. The strappy black sandals are a different matter. My feet are dainty in comparison to my frame, and the longer I've known Matt, the more convinced I've become that he has a fetish for them. He often talks about making me walk round the house all day, naked but for these heels. One day, I ought to tell him how little persuasion that would involve.

I take one last look at myself in the mirror, reveling in how slutty I look. That woman at the checkout would be disgusted, I'm sure, by the way the nightdress fails to conceal my heavy breasts, my fleshy thighs, the prominent swell of my belly. But I'm not wearing this for her benefit. I'm wearing it for Matt's, and he loves every last voluptuous inch of me.

Even so, his reaction when I pluck the console handset from his grasp verges on the comical. "Fuck me!" he exclaims, his Welsh accent pronounced even more than usual, as he takes in the sight of me, in all my nylon-clad magnificence. "Do women still really wear those things? I thought the last one withered and died when they stopped making *Carry On* films." He rises from the couch, his rapidly rising cock already threatening to push through the fly of his underwear. "You look amazing, mind."

"Is everything ready?" I ask, trying not to laugh at his eagerness. Funny how I'm dressed like the archetypal submissive sex symbol, yet suddenly I have all the control. That will change soon enough, but for now, I'm happy to let Matt bustle round, taking all the supplies I bought earlier into the guest bedroom.

Plastic sheeting already covers the bed—which has been stripped of all coverings, bar the bottom sheet—and the carpet. This is going to get messy, and the sheeting will cut down on the amount of cleanup later.

Without being prompted, I take up my position, lying back on the cool, slightly clammy plastic. As Matt watches, I spread my legs, revealing my freshly shaved pussy through the split in the cheap panties, its beauty emphasized by the ugly nylon ruffles. A dish of peaches lies on the bedside table. I bite into one, just as sensuously as Matt did earlier with the strawberry. Sticky juice spills out, dribbling down the side of my mouth. It tastes so good, but it does nothing to sate my appetite.

Matt peels off his T-shirt, then advances on me, cock rigid and poking free of his shorts. Taking the top off the tub of custard, he drizzles a slow trail down my neck and over my breasts. Almost before I've registered its coldness, Matt's hot mouth is on my skin, licking it up.

Moving lower, he mouths my nipple through the nightdress, mashing the nylon wetly to my body and making me moan.

Not satisfied with that, he grabs the neckline of the babydoll and tugs sharply, ripping the thin fabric in two. When my breasts are bare, he reaches for the clotted cream, massaging a big, gooey handful onto each one.

That's when the doorbell rings.

"Who the hell's that?" I ask.

"Dunno. I'll just check." Matt rises from the bed and looks out of the window, down on whomever's standing on the drive below. "It's Will," he announces before opening the window wide and yelling, "All right, Will mate. We're up here. Let yourself in. It's not locked."

"You can't be serious." Even as I speak, I can hear the sound of the front door opening. Will is the team's star fly-half and is Matt's closest friend at the club, and they've long worked on the principle of *Mi casa es su casa*, popping in and out of each other's homes pretty much whenever they feel like it. I'd never had a problem with the arrangement—until now.

Matt goes to the half-open bedroom door and calls down the stairs. "Come on up, why don't you?" Turning back to me with a grin, he says, "He must have finally finished the last level on *Zombie Aftermath*. He said he'd bring it round when he had."

"And you've let him in the house with his stupid video game when we're—" I don't get the chance to let Matt know what I really think, because at that moment, Will pushes open the door and walks in to see me on the bed in my torn, slutty nightdress, naked tits lavishly smeared with clotted cream. His initially startled expression gives way to something suggesting he's already more comfortable with the situation than I am.

After a long moment, he quips, "Tell me, do those things taste as good as they look?"

"Why don't you find out, mate?" Matt replies. "Eva doesn't mind, do you, love?"

Mutely, I shake my head. The truth is that now, I'm getting used to the fact that Will has blundered in on our messy games, and I really don't mind if he joins in. Matt and I have often discussed the idea of bringing a third person into our bed, but until now, it's never been anything more than a fantasy. After all, how do you seriously go about organizing such a scenario? And all other considerations aside, Will is properly gorgeous, built on leaner lines than Matt but just as beautifully muscular, with limpid dark eyes and an angular bone structure that has so far escaped unscathed from the hurly-burly of rugby.

As Will kicks off his deck shoes so he can climb onto the bed beside me, I'm just a little surprised by the obvious lust in his eyes. For as long as I've known him, all the girls he's dated have been blond and tiny. I got on well with Adele, his last girl-friend; she might have been no more than eight stone wringing wet, but she was feisty and funny. And she wasn't one of those women who pushes a salad round her plate and calls it eating, so of course we were going to get on. Given the evidence, I'd simply assumed Will's tastes invariably ran to type, but as his hands caress my big, cream-covered tits, I'm starting to think I might have read him wrong.

"Mmm, gorgeous," he sighs, pushing my breasts together so he can admire the deep, enticing cleavage between them. "God, Eva, I'd love to slide my cock between those."

"So why don't you?" I ask. "But you might want to take some of those clothes off first."

His scramble to get naked is so frantic I almost laugh. But the sight of him, stripped and ready, stills that impulse. He's tanned the same dark-honey shade all over, and his cock rises up, smooth and hard, from a patch of hair that's been trimmed down to al-most nothing, making him look larger than he already is.

For the first time, I realize I've not been paying any atten-tion to Matt in all this. I glance round to see he's drawn the stool that normally sits beneath the dressing table close to the bed. The best seat in the house, for a performance he's long dreamed of. He sits, munching on the half-eaten peach with obvious relish, as Will straddles my body, hard-on bobbing proudly in front of him.

Appetizing as it looks in its natural state, it needs a little extra lubrication if it's going to slide smoothly between my tits. Reaching for the chocolate sauce, I squirt a generous amount over my cleavage. Will presents his cock to me, and I wrap the soft, heavy flesh of my breasts around it.

The action is greeted by a chorus of groans—one from Will, as the coolness of the sauce meets his hot length, and another from Matt, watching and wanking his own erection.

Will starts to fuck my cleavage, slightly awkwardly at first, but soon getting into a rhythm. Whenever the head—glistening with a mixture of pre-come and chocolate sauce—pops out from between my tits, I lick it, enjoying the salty-sweet taste. From the blissful expression on Will's face, he could happily let me do this until he comes, but I'm thinking of my own needs.

Catching hold of his slippery cock, I suck it until most of the sauce is gone. Will's lost in the sensation, loving the feeling of being lodged in the tightness of my throat. All I can hear from Matt is the steady shuffling of his palm—no doubt slippery with peach juice—up and down his shaft.

Eventually, to Will's obvious disappointment, I stop and let him slip from my lips. "Condom, please, Matt," I say, wiping a trickle of chocolate from the corner of my mouth.

Obediently, Matt hands over a foil-wrapped package. Mint-flavored, I can't help but notice as Will rolls the thin green latex into place. Not that I'll be tasting it, of course. There's a pulse beating strongly between my legs, a molten heat in my swollen pussy lips. In the crudest, most basic terms, I need to be fucked, and I'm not too shy to let Will know that.

"Let me have you from behind," he says. "I need to see that lovely big ass of yours jiggling as I fuck you."

I'm not one to turn down a request like that—not when I know it means his cock will slide into me all the more deeply—so I get up on all fours, just like he asks.

"Okay, better lose this, sweetheart." With that, Will rips the already tattered nightdress the rest of the way off. He leaves the panties on, though. Maybe he likes the way they draw attention to the urgent red pout of my sex poking out from between my legs.

Before he enters me, he slaps my ass. Not hard enough to hurt; he just wants to see my cheeks wobble under his palm. I've always known Matt loves my curves, but having Will admire them, too, is a real boost. But then I can't imagine that any woman, no matter what her size, could fail to feel anything less than totally desirable in the presence of her partner and his best friend, both of them totally aroused and ready to fuck her.

Will's hands roam over my hips, my thighs, cupping and squeezing, feeling and adoring. My fingers somehow find themselves at my crotch, idly stroking my clit. Giddy pleasure ripples through me—the first step on the ascent to orgasm. The sight of me playing with myself like this spurs Will on to part my lips with those long, clever fingers that handle a rugby ball so adeptly. I feel his cock pushing inside me, making its hefty presence felt. Matt is urging him on, telling him to fuck me really hard. Team player to the end, Will does as he's told.

Once I'm used to the feel of Will's thick shaft sliding back and forth, his hands gripping my ample hips as he thrusts into me over and over, I beckon Matt close. He may be having a good time just watching, but I want him to take a more active part in the proceedings.

Matt doesn't object when I grab his cock and feed it between my lips. Indeed, he picks up the pot of clotted cream and slathers a handful along his shaft. The chimes of a passing ice-cream van float in through the open window, playing a tinny version of "Greensleeves." I'm sure nothing that van sells tastes as good as the way Matt does now, the sweetness of the cream mixing with the briny essence of hard, excited man-flesh. *If this is greediness*, I think, *if this makes me a bad girl, then bring it on*, because the truth is, I could gorge on this delicious confection forever.

Will's in me so deeply his groin bangs against my ass cheeks with each thrust. I'm so full, at both ends, yet I'm ravenous for more.

It's Will who peaks first, yelling like he's scored a match-winning try as he comes. The audible proof of his orgasm, twinned with the wicked persistence of my tongue, can't help but push Matt over the edge. My taste buds register the bitter tang of his come—another distinct flavor on top of everything else I've swallowed this evening—but it still doesn't satisfy me. Only when fingers—Will's, Matt's, I'm too far gone to be sure, and anyway, I no longer know if it matters—rub at my clit does my world dissolve into the sweetest, creamiest of climaxes.

We collapse together—a panting, satisfied man on each side of me and hands still gently stroking my breasts and belly as we search for, and fail to find, the words to adequately describe just how good that was.

While Will's in the shower, cleaning off the last of the chocolate sauce before he leaves for home, Matt turns to me.

"I suppose it's confession time," he says.

I wait for him to elaborate, unsure what's coming next.

"Will actually finished the video game two days ago. He was going to bring it round then, but I told him to wait until tonight."

"So you set this whole thing up between you?" I don't know whether to go ballistic at Matt or, given the fantastic threesome we've just enjoyed, applaud him for his ingenuity.

"Not really. He had no idea that when he turned up he'd find us in bed, but I thought that if he did, he'd be well up for joining in—and I was right."

I stop his words with a deep, tongue-probing kiss, and this time, it's a display of pure gratitude. As I said, I have a big appetite—and Matt seems to have discovered the perfect way of satisfying it.

In the Early Morning Light

BY KRISTINA WRIGHT

This is how it begins. Me lying in bed just before dawn, woozy from a lack of sleep, praying (though I am not religious) for twenty more minutes of rest. Thirty minutes would be better. I roll over on my side, because I can't get comfortable on my back, and my breasts are too swollen to sleep on my stomach. Still not comfortable, I close my eyes anyway. Beggars can't be choosers.

I feel his arm curve over my hip as he nestles into the space behind me. His hand strokes my belly—soft, warm and doughy, with a scar above my pubic area that is not as red and raw-looking as it was a few weeks ago—and I sigh in frustration. I just want to sleep.

I don't like him touching me. I don't like anyone touching me. My body is not my body—it hasn't been for months and months. First it belonged to the creature growing inside it, stretching it to maximum capacity. Now it belongs to the baby I birthed just nine weeks ago—the baby still sleeping in the next room the way I want to be sleeping right now. The baby who will be awake soon, screaming and wriggling and demanding, latching onto breasts that don't produce enough milk to nourish him, despite their size. I try to remember if I made any bottles of formula before I fell into bed at 3 AM. I can't recall.

I want to squirm away as he moves his hand up to cup one tender breast, but there is nowhere for me to go, and besides, I'm too tired. Too tired to move, too tired to give him what he wants, too tired to think. Bone tired. No one ever told me I'd be this tired.

"Don't," I whisper, my voice barely audible for fear of waking the baby. "I'm tired."

"Me, too, sweetheart. Me, too," he says gently, though he doesn't stop touching me, doesn't move away.

His fingers pluck at my nipples—gently, because he knows they're sensitive and sore from being put into service several times a day. He loves my breasts and thinks they're beautiful. I loathe them, because they're swollen and misshapen and riddled with stretch marks and are inadequate to feed my child. But his gentle touch stirs something inside me, and my breast responds, sending a few drops of precious fluid over the tip.

I moan in frustration. He assumes it is arousal, because he reaches farther along my rounded body and inflicts the same gentle touch on my other nipple. There is no milk this time; this breast is dry and useless. But it still responds to his touch, the dark nipple tightening with excitement.

This time, my moan is one of pleasure.

He palms my breast, massages it gently before releasing it and slipping his hand down to my flabby belly, stroking the rolls that were once taut skin from the growing baby inside. I never had abs to admire, but at least they were there—muscles to pull in the flab. The muscles have been cut and no longer care to hold anything in. Between the scar and my belly button is a dead zone—I feel nothing there except that peculiar sensation of weight if I'm leaning against something. The area is numb from the surgery and might always be, but I know his hand is there, running along the ridges of purple marks. "Badges of honor," my mother calls them. What does she know? She didn't have stretch marks with any of her four pregnancies.

He's still touching me, still not taking the hint that I just want to be left alone. I cringe in revulsion, wondering why I didn't slip on a T-shirt before I crawled into bed. The answer is simple, of course: After feeding the baby what little milk I had and supplementing with another two ounces of formula, I was too tired to put on a T-shirt. I was almost too tired to walk down the hall to the bedroom, and I might have curled up in the chair in the nursery and gone to sleep if not for the fear that I might snore and wake the baby.

I have told him that I am the opposite of touch-deprived; that having a newborn has made me touch-overloaded. Even the gentlest of touches, even a hug or backrub, feels like sharp nails on a fresh sunburn. I don't want to be touched, but some part of me still longs for the connection of touch, to know I am more than a mother, than a milk-maker, than a Frankenstein's monster of stretch marks and skin discolorations and numb flesh and that ugly scar.

"Let me," he whispers, as if sensing the war going on inside me. The minutes are ticking away.

He slips his hand beneath the waistband of my panties and rests two fingers on my slit. He has not touched this part of me in over five months. Three months of pelvic rest followed by two months of postpartum recovery, recommended by my doctor, despite the cesarean delivery. That was something else they didn't tell me—that I would bleed for several weeks, even if I didn't deliver the baby vaginally. The bleeding has long since stopped, and I got the green light to resume sexual activity at my postpartum checkup, so we could have had sex by now if I had wanted to. But I hadn't.

He does not move his fingers; he just leaves them there, straddling my pussy lips. I am freshly shaven—well, it's been two days, but that's still fresh for me. I didn't shave in anticipation of having sex or because he prefers me that way, but because the hair that had grown back since the birth had been driving me crazy. I often awoke (when I was able to sleep) scratching myself. So out of practicality, I shaved. I'm all about practicality these days. It's called survival.

I may be tired, but my newly bare pussy is responding to the fingers touching it for the first time in five months. I have masturbated a few times since the bleeding stopped, always with my vibrator, because it is the quickest (and therefore most practical) way, mostly to help me fall asleep (again with the practicality), and always when he was in the shower or feeding the baby. I didn't want him to think it was an invitation for him to do more. But now my pussy is issuing its own invitation, moistening under the weight of his still fingers, becoming swollen.

"Is this okay?" he asks, bringing his fingers together so that they press against my opening and my now-engorged clitoris.

What do I say? No? Stop? I don't want to have sex with you ever again? Let me sleep, goddammit? All of the above?

I say what my pussy wants me to say. "It's okay. Yes, it's okay."

His touch remains slow, lazy, as if we have all the time in the world, even though we don't. He dips his fingers into my pussy, gathers some moisture there, and drags his fingertips over my clit. I shiver. Vibrators are lovely, efficient things, but they do not compare to the touch of someone who knows me and my body. The best part is, I don't have to do it for myself. I can lay there and let him get me off. If I were a good and selfless lover, I'd reach behind me and return the favor, stroke his growing erection as it presses against my ass. But my days are spent being a selfless mother, and I have nothing left to give him. So I am selfish. I let him touch me, and I simply enjoy it.

"Yes," I whisper to my pillow. "More. Keep touching me."

Despite my exhaustion, my hips begin to move on their own, finding a rhythm I thought my body had forgotten. He moans behind me, presses against me. I feel something like feminine pride blossoming, the way my pussy is swelling and opening.

He moves his hand from my pussy to fumble between us. He is freeing his cock from his boxers. I debate what to do. I had hoped he would just get me off, give me a quick little orgasm so I could get fifteen, maybe twenty minutes of sleep. It crosses my mind that if I give him what he wants, maybe he'll get up and feed the baby, and I could buy myself another hour. *An hour!*

This is what new parenthood has done to me. I consider bartering my body for more sleep. Me, who used to want to fuck all the time.

But then he's there, nestled in the crack of my ass, warm and hard and familiar, and I'm wiggling again, even while I'm trying to figure out what I can get away with and how to squeeze out a few minutes of rest.

"Baby, you're driving me crazy," he murmurs, kissing my neck. His cheek is rough with stubble, and his voice sounds as tired as I feel. This hasn't been easy for him either. But his body is still his body; he still looks the same, if a little more tired and disheveled. Nothing a shower and a shave and a cup of coffee won't cure—and I can't even have coffee because I'm still trying to breastfeed.

I reach behind me and rub him. I'm startled by how strange it feels to touch him like this. We'd fucked like rabbits right up until I started spotting, and my doctor said no more sex until after the baby came. Even then, I'd given him blowjobs and handjobs, because regardless of what my doctor said, I was still horny as hell. But not being able to have intercourse and being told I shouldn't even give myself an orgasm put a damper on my sex drive.

But here it is again, waking up, even while I feel like I am swimming through a fog of exhaustion.

I angle my hips down and back, pressing my ass against him as I guide him to my entrance. I don't have the energy to get on top of him, and I don't want him on top of me, compressing my belly—or worse, looking at me—but this, this I can do. I feel the head of his cock nudge between my swollen lips. He moans when he feels the warm wetness inside, waiting for him.

"Oh, Carolyn, baby, you feel so good."

I whimper in reply. He feels wonderful inside me, filling me as he slides into me slowly. The benefit of a cesarean delivery is no pain during intercourse—no tender incision, no tearing, just blissful pleasure.

He grips my hips and pulls me back on his cock until he is fully seated inside me. I let out a long, low moan. This—*this*—is what I've been missing. Our position is too awkward for anything more than slow, languid lovemaking, but I still yearn for more.

"Harder," I whisper. "I want you harder."

He responds by lifting my leg and draping it over his hip. Holding onto my thigh for leverage, he begins to fuck me with long, driving strokes. My breasts bounce against each other, my stomach jiggles in a comic way, my ass slaps noisily against his thighs and stomach with every stroke, but I don't care. For the first time in months, I'm not focused on any other part of my body except my pussy. And while the rest of me may have expanded and shifted in ways that might never return to normal or feel completely familiar, my pussy is wet and aroused and very, very much *mine*.

"Yes," I whimper, slipping my hand down between my thighs to manipulate my clit while he fucks me. "Fuck me, Sam."

And he does. Where his touch has been gentle before—solicitous through pregnancy and postpartum recovery, nonsexual when helping me maneuver the baby to my breast—now he is rough, demanding, selfish. My skin tingles where he touches me, grabs me, still gentle with my breasts but firm with my hips, ass, shoulders, thighs. He pulls my leg higher and covers my hand with his own, both of us sliding our fingers along my wet slit, toying with my clit, stroking his cock as it slides in and out of me. Panting, sweaty, fucking like we haven't fucked since—

The unmistakable sound of baby Henry waking up brings everything to a halt. Sam goes still inside me, and I bite back a cry of frustration as I strain to listen. The baby monitor next to the bed echoes the sounds from down the hall—a cry, followed by a whimper. Then . . . quiet snuffling sighs.

"Do you think . . . ?"

"*Shhhh,*" I say in response to Sam's question. I fondle my neglected clit and push my ass back toward him. "Just fuck me before he's really awake."

Sam chuckles, but he doesn't argue. As if resetting the hands on a clock, he resumes his hard, steady thrusts inside me. We are quieter now, more conscious of the baby who will awaken any minute, but the passion is no less. I bite my lip to keep from moaning as I rub my clit with frantic strokes, aching for the kind of release I haven't enjoyed in forever.

Burying his head in the curve of my neck to muffle his own moans, Sam quickens his thrusts. He is close. So am I. I arch against him as the dual touch of our fingers and the sensation of his cock rubbing me just the right way bring my orgasm crashing over me. My pussy tightens around his girth, and that is all it takes for him to join me, both of us gasping and moaning as quietly as possible, riding out the powerful release we were almost denied. He squeezes my hand as it rests over my mound, and I gasp, my clit sensitive and still throbbing.

The sun is fully up now, shining on the bed as wetness pools under us. His. Mine. Ours. I whimper as he slips his cock free of my pussy, feeling empty and bereft. Though it has been months, my body remembers that feeling, and now, even though I am sated, it wants more.

As if reading my mind, Sam squeezes my hand again, sending a shiver up my spine as my pussy clenches in response. "Soon, baby," he promises. "When Henry is sleeping through the night, we're going to be spending a lot of time in bed *not* sleeping."

Henry's soft snuffles become louder, and turn into full-fledged wails. I sigh and start to get out of bed, feeling a twinge of pain between my thighs as my tender pussy protests. Sam clasps my wrist and pulls me back down, nuzzling his face against my breasts.

"I have to feed him," I say, my voice weary with exhaustion even while maternal need quickens my pulse.

"Stay in bed and rest for awhile." Sam gets out of bed and adjusts his boxers. "I'll feed him."

I laugh, thinking better of telling him about the mental conversation I had with myself before we had sex. "Thanks, honey," I tell him, pulling the quilt over me and tucking my hand under my cheek as he leaves our bedroom to take care of the baby.

That's how it began. Nothing has changed, really. And yet everything has. I am myself again. Or, if not myself, my newly discovered self. My sexy, soft, fuckable, maternal self.

I smile and close my eyes. It is going to be the best nap of my life.

See and Be Seen
BY ARLETTE BRAND

It was so unexpected. Her eyes fluttered before they focused on what she thought she'd seen.

There, outside her open second-story window, twenty feet away—in the apartment building behind her own, and on the very same floor—a man sat on the edge of his bed, looking out his window at her. The light from his ceiling cast a harsh glow, and his face fell partly in shadow. *Almost like a skull,* she thought, his brow casting his eyes into twin dark hollows.

She expected him to flinch and mirror her own sense of surprise, but he didn't. He sat coolly in his white undershirt and boxer shorts, his elbows resting on his open thighs, his hands dropped languidly into the space between.

Terese let out a little gasp and hopped away from the window.

She knew he hadn't really *seen* anything. She'd undressed with the window wide open, but she had her clever routine. She stood with her back to the window, pulling her dress swiftly over her head and bringing her arms behind her back to unhook her bra. Then she yanked her nightshirt over her head and tugged it over her breasts before spinning back around, fully covered.

Terese never expected to see anyone at that window. For a long time she assumed the entire second floor of that building was vacant. Lights seldom glowed from within, and the shades were always pulled.

Despite his stillness and plain gaze, Terese didn't feel as frightened as she thought she should. She didn't feel violated, as another woman might. What made her move out of sight was modesty and embarrassment.

The modesty felt distinctly childlike—a mild shame left over from childhood, the kind of fleeting horror felt by a five-year-old girl upon discovering she's been seen in her underpants.

Well, some *little girls.* Terese thought of her best friend back home, Anna-Marie. Anna-Marie, who'd been boy crazy since preschool. Terese could still recall Anna-Marie as a lanky first-grader, doing running jumps onto the laps of any teenage boys who'd let her. Terese's own mother would occasionally be a witness to this and would chastise little Anna, pulling her away from the boys and men with nervous urgency. Anna-Marie was apt to straddle things and ride them, even the rigid thighs of seated ladies who'd let her. Terese thought it curious but didn't understand why it pleasured her friend until years later. It was a telling preview of the sexually attuned teenager and young woman Anna would become.

Terese was not only plagued with a sense of sexual propriety but she was also ashamed of her body. She'd gained fifty pounds since graduating from high school a decade before, and her hips were too wide and her belly too thick to camouflage—not to say Terese didn't try. She dressed in a uniform of ankle-length hippie dresses with a man's oversized blazer thrown over them, even in sweltering weather. The ensemble covered her flaws while still giving her a sense of who she thought she was: a creative type, quirky.

She dared to swivel her head around to see if the man was still watching her. The rectangle of his window was dark. She pulled her own shade closed and turned on the television.

⚬⚭✦⚮⚬

The next night, as she rode the bus home from her evening class, Terese found herself thinking about the man across the alley. The bus engine made her seat vibrate, and she felt a quick contraction deep inside. The rosy folds of her pussy were getting wet and sliding against each other, and the sensation pleased her.

Terese thought of her own body parading before the window, under the spotlight of a bright, cheap ceiling fixture. Part of her wanted to cringe—or rather, part of her felt she *should* want to cringe. With a body like hers, shouldn't she want to cringe? But somehow, imagining herself under the gaze of this intent observer, her body became a lush and wanted thing.

He hadn't looked away when her dress came off and revealed how her back fat folded over the elastic of her poorly fitting bra. The width of her behind, framed by her own window, hadn't sent him fleeing. He looked—and kept on looking. He filled his eyes with her form. Whether or not he'd admit it to his friends the next day, this man—in the quiet of that late July bedroom, in the hours when working people fell into easy comas in the flickering blue light of televisions, in a corner of the city where the aroma of nearby flowering hedges competed with freeway exhaust, where the night air lay upon the skin like heavy ointment—here, this living, breathing man was watching *her body.*

Terese liked it.

꧁ ❧ ꧂

She opened her bedroom door and flipped on the light switch, pretending she didn't notice his window lit like honey. She saw his shadow move across his stark white wall, then watched as his pale blue boxers moved into view, and he settled onto the bed. His legs hung over the side, and he leaned forward, as though removing his socks. It was taking him an unreasonably long time.

Terese discovered a secret angle at which she could watch him through her dresser mirror while appearing not to notice him at all. When her back was turned, he promptly sat up and turned his head to watch her. He sat perfectly still.

Terese's heart thudded against her diaphragm. Her stomach trembled.

She recognized, oh so clearly, that she *wanted* him to see her.

But no, Terese thought again. It wasn't his passive observance that she wanted. She wanted to be the one *showing him.*

This wasn't like her. She'd never been into voyeurism. *What's going on with me?* she wondered. Few things turned her on—*really* turned her on—and it frustrated her. In high school, Anna-Marie had been able to get excited over the most uninspiring things. A shirtless model on a campy birthday card, for example. Terese envied her for it. Even when she masturbated, Terese had to work so hard to arouse herself, she usually fell asleep exhausted before she could come.

But this was a throbbing, ready thing she'd seldom felt before. *This was what it must feel like to be Anna-Marie.* It felt as though a stream of lava ran from Terese's solar plexus and into her panties. She had a frightening, primal urge to drop to her knees, spread her legs open as wide as they'd go, like a gymnast or a contortionist, nearly touching her pussy to the carpet, and *give birth* to her orgasm. She felt she might drop a balloon out of her, a balloon full and hanging low and swollen with white-hot water.

She slid her jacket off her arms and tossed it onto the sofa.

The man continued to watch. Still.

She stood so her body was perfectly framed by the window, centered, and stood with her legs apart. She felt powerful this way. Showcased. She rolled her shoulders back and looked down at her breasts and belly, each protruding with a curve meant to fill a hand, or two hands, or more. Protruding roundnesses, like the trembling, near-bursting water balloon that rested so tentatively inside her throbbing vagina.

She gathered up the skirt of her dress and pulled it over her head. She reached high, high enough to feel a long, delicious, aching stretch in her arms. She tossed the dress to the floor.

Her hips were tilted back, setting her ass at a high angle, and she could feel him getting an eyeful of her plain white cotton panties.

Suddenly she had the urge to feel her own ass cheeks naked to the air. She knew that even if he wasn't there to watch her, even if he walked away, she'd still need to feel her ass bare, *now*—with her window wide and gaping at the brick of his building, at the rows of other windows, at the sly grin of the crescent moon. She slipped her palms into her panties and stroked her own velvet flesh before pulling them down. Not off, but down, to gather just under the fullest part of her rear end, suggesting themselves so close to her weeping, wanting opening.

In the mirror, the man straightened his back and continued to watch.

Casual, like a body that had known only perfection, sauntering back and forth across a locker room and stirring envy. Terese reached behind her back and began to unhook her bra but pivoted with faux innocence so he could see her breasts from the side as they sprung from her falling bra. She ran her fingertips along the smiling curve of them, then circled her nipples with her thumbs. She imagined him suddenly a fourteen-year-old boy, wondering, *Are they supposed to do that? Does it feel good? Is that one of those girl things, from health class?* She laughed a little.

Terese continued to circle her nipples, as though with a sense of purpose. As though it was something to be done. A sort of sexual maintenance. She tipped her head back slightly and let her mouth drop open, to show she enjoyed it. To show how easily she could invoke this pleasure, how ripe and young and ready she was. This touching, this release—it was something a girl needed to do.

Terese opened her eyes, and her attention landed on her desk chair. It was an armless swivel chair with rough, burlaplike, gray upholstery. She moved toward it, stood above it.

She pulled her panties down her legs and tossed them off with one foot. Then she straddled the chair backward, balanced on her forefeet, and lowered herself over it.

The pink flesh between her legs was slack and moist and hypersensitive. She detected every raised nub in the fabric, every tiny corkscrew fiber rising from the surface. She pressed her weight downward through the floor of her pelvis, staining the seat cushion with her moisture. She rocked her hips forward and back, delighted by the smoothness of her own movements. The weight and round-ness of her own bottom charmed her, the cheeks spreading and lift-ing, again and again, as she rocked. In her head, she heard a voice, startlingly similar to her own, moaning, *Oh, how I love this ass*.

The chair became the face of a man with late-day stubble. She teased it, brushing it lightly, then hovering, torturing him—or torturing her? Then she ground herself into it, deliciously rough and yet forgiving, supportive yet surrendering to her own contours.

Terese arched her back and felt the peculiar kiss of the air, hot and present, against her erect nipples. Like a mouth, she thought. The temperature difference was subtle. Summer air mak-ing itself known to her breasts, like twin mouths open wide and round, *O*, lowering themselves wet and toothless over her rosy nipples. She let go a sound, *Oohh*.

She sensed his eyes rolling over her curves, hungrily memo-rizing the succulent quiver of her breasts. She wanted something inside. So, so badly.

She rose from the chair. She walked to her dresser and

leaned over with her hand on the edge, legs spread wide, bent deep at the waist. She watched him in the mirror now without averting her eyes.

The rigidity of his body was a tonic to Terese. He was captivated. Overcome. Unable to be torn from the sight of her. The building might crumble around him and he'd remain riveted on her form, panting. She noticed the shadow of his Adam's apple rising and falling on his neck. His attention scorched her skin like a nearing inferno. It was a phantom arm that reached up inside of her and stroked and beckoned.

She reached down and inserted four fingers inside and began to reach, reach, reach for that place he had touched from a distance. At the depths, she began to smart in the most delicious way. She whimpered. Inside she imagined a trampoline, scarlet as a tart's lipstick. It was littered with little girls, landing hard and jumping with all their might, getting flung upward again. They chanted: *Higher! Higher! Higher!* Their skirts flew high above their heads, obscuring their faces, revealing rose-print underpants with a satin rosette at the waistline.

This was something a girl had to do. With one leg balanced awkwardly on the edge of a drawer, it was both curious and necessary.

Terese came hard. Moisture cascaded over her hand; a droplet traced a slow path around her wrist. She choked from her deepest throat. She seethed and sputtered. Every breath was a hot blast of wind. A perfume bottle fell on its side. The lace table runner slipped and hung limply off the dresser.

She stood now, bent and exhausted, still gripping the furniture.

She looked into the mirror, past the snakelike strands of her hair sticking to her dewy face, past her flushed cheeks and white shoulders and softening nipples.

Yes, he was still there. But standing this time. Standing, and close to his window screen.

Terese ran her palms slowly down the sides of her torso, following a fascinating road over the swell of her hips. Her full thighs touched one another and were sugary-sticky.

Then she turned to face the window.

She looked right at him.

With slow surety, she approached the window, hands dangling, relaxed at her sides.

His undershirt and boxers were gone now. His face was more apparent here, a little closer to her, and the light from above was less direct. He was ordinary-looking. Inoffensive. The kind of man your mom might want you to meet.

Terese did her best to connect with his gaze.

He reached down and took himself in his hands.

Big Girls Do Cry

BY RACHEL KRAMER BUSSEL

You would not believe the number of men who think that just because I'm a big girl—a voluptuous size 16 who isn't afraid to show off all my assets—that what I'm put on this earth for is to beat their bottoms silly. I'm sure there are plenty of women who get off on that—because I've seen them in action and heard plenty of stories—but having a naked, eager, collared man at my feet just isn't for me. I'm not offended by it or anything; it just doesn't turn me on, just like some people prefer rocky road and some prefer vanilla. I like my road to be rocky—as long as someone else is doing the rocking.

I prefer to be the one on the floor, stripped bare, eagerly waiting for whatever the perfect, sexy, handsome, smart, mind-fucking, sadistic dom of my dreams wants me to do. I've been like this for as long as I can remember; the rush of having a lover give me even the merest instruction, kinky or not—from "kiss my hand" to "show me your panties"—is enough to turn me into a puddle of mush. When I get like that, all hot and liquid, my body feels, in a way, weightless. Not literally, of course, and a size 0 is not something I aspire to; I mean a more ethereal kind of weightless, like I'm floating and then being brought back down to earth with a loud, painful, delicious smack on my ass.

Yet for all my desires, it's only happened twice. Only two men have been able to see exactly how I want to be treated and have been capable of delivering it. I get that dominance isn't for everyone—if it were, my attempts to shimmy into a corset and latex skirt and slash a whip in the air would've by now led me either to a devoted husband or to a career as a dominatrix. But for the most part, I've spent my time in the kinky world watching and waiting. I've always believed that good things come to those who wait, as facile as that might sound. I'm twenty-four, and I've been waiting long enough—observing, staring, lusting after those women lucky enough to get taken over a man's knee, to be tied up to a cross, to have a gag shoved in their mouths while they thrash around, knowing that they can't escape until everyone gets what they need.

I know what I want—to cry, to scream, to struggle, to surrender, to be "forced" into all manner of degrading scenarios—but I don't just want it from anyone. That's why those two brief dalliances were just that—something about what we were doing didn't feel quite right. The motions were there, sure, but the men seemed to be either taking out some latent anger on me or simply going through the motions. I want a man who means it. I don't want it from men who hold a lurking undercurrent of misogyny, who think the scene is a place to let that loose. I don't want men who'll try to "order" me to lose weight and think that's okay because they're the top and whatever they say goes. I don't want a man who doesn't respect every inch of my womanhood, but rather one who wants to top me, torture me, and tie me up because he respects my every curvy pound.

For a long time, I hated this need and tried to subvert it, going out with vanilla boys who were perfectly sweet and sweetly perfect. And therein lay the problem. They were too sweet, too soft, and they treated me too tenderly. Or they somehow fetishized my size, turning me into a woman to put on a pedestal and cower under. If it wasn't men building me up to an inflated size and importance, like in René Magritte's painting *The Giantess*, they were considering me a cuddly teddy bear of a girl, someone whose cleavage they could nuzzle up to, someone they could stroke and fondle, someone who could mommy them in a sexual way, but someone they would never slap and sting. That would offend their principles. I say fuck principles, fuck propriety. What's a hot-blooded kinky girl to do with her desire to bend over?

❧☙❧

The answer, apparently, was "wait." Patience is a virtue and all that, though I don't consider myself particularly virtuous. I don't believe in knights in shining armor, or sleek leather, or anything like that, but I have to tell you, when I met Todd, everything just clicked.

We were standing in line at a concert—Adele, if you want to know. I was there by myself, because her music is so beautiful, I

knew I'd cry, and I didn't want to do that in front of even my closest friends. Sometimes the best music is enough to fill you up, and
her voice struck me in the center of my chest.

I was smashed into the middle of the crowd and only had
eyes for Adele. When she sang "Someone Like You," I let the tears
flow. I'd never lost a man like the girl in the song, but I'd dreamt
about the man who'd give me all of himself in return for all of me.
It wasn't until the encore that Todd and I made eyes. He smiled,
an almost shy smile. He was tall, with shaggy brown hair, and wore
a black T-shirt and well-worn pale blue jeans, which hung loosely
from his lanky frame. He wasn't exactly my type. This big girl goes
for even bigger guys—ones who look like James Gandolfini when I
want a bad boy and John Goodman when I don't. But it was Todd's
face that drew me in.

He wasn't crying, but he looked like he'd been sucker-
punched by the music just as much as I had. We stepped slightly
closer as Adele sang her final songs and bid us goodbye, and I just
stood there, not wanting to leave and ruin the magic. "Beautiful,
isn't she?" he asked softly. I looked up at him and noticed his
long eyelashes. There was something girly about him, which made
what happened afterward so ironic.

"Yeah," I said. "I could've stayed here all night."

"Want to maybe get a drink, see if we can find her on a
jukebox somewhere?"

One drink turned into three, followed by two sodas. We
ended up shutting down the bar (which turned out not to have
a jukebox). We'd started out sitting across from each other in a
booth, and then gradually, I'd moved next to him, inching closer
and closer. He was smart and funny and sweet, but not all sweet.

There was a glint of something dark in those gorgeous hazel eyes that made me tingle all over.

"So, what now?" he asked, leaving it up to me. I was sitting on the side of the booth closest to the exit, and I stood. As I lifted my purse onto my shoulder, he stood, and his hand brushed against my ass. The heat from his touch traveled all the way through me. I shifted back toward him, hoping, despite my earlier tiredness, that the electricity sparking through my dress and panties directly into my skin meant what I thought it did. He stayed still, and I pressed farther back, until his fingers cupped my skin just so, giving me a squeeze that was gentle but firm enough to make me moan.

He leaned over and blew on the back of my neck, and tendrils of hair that had strayed from my ponytail tickled against my skin.

"Amy," he said. "Turn around."

I did, and we stood face to face, his arm wrapped around me, still cupping my face. I was close enough to feel how hard he was. "Tell me what you want." His words were soft, almost like the time I went to a hypnotist. But he wanted to hear me, wanted me to share exactly what I was thinking.

I had to shut my eyes, the heat rushing to my cheeks as I took a deep breath and said, "I want you to spank me. No panties. Over your knee. I want you to make me scream." I opened my eyes, which were now wet with tears of desire; I hadn't realized how arousing it would be to say those words, an arousal directly in proportion to my fear.

"Have you ever been spanked like that before, Amy?"

"No, not like that, just a few slaps. Taps, really. They weren't enough." It got a little easier to say the words; that time, I looked at him.

"You want the pain, don't you, Amy?" he asked, tightening his hold on my ass.

"Yes," I gasped as his hand blatantly palmed my cheek before dipping lower.

"Bend over this table then. Show me how much you want it. If you don't, I won't believe you truly need it."

I knew there were a few stragglers left in the bar, and that the staff wanted us to leave, but I couldn't help it—I bent over. I lay my face directly on the cold, sticky table, my ass sticking up in the air, the outline of my panties surely visible to Todd and possibly others. I like bikinis, which give pretty full coverage, but I could tell they had bunched between my legs, where I was wet and swollen.

Todd stepped behind me and again cupped my cheeks, using both hands. He massaged my ass gently at first, then more firmly, occasionally stroking lightly over my pussy. It was thrilling and unnerving to be so blatantly bent over. He did that for maybe thirty seconds, but they were thirty of the most thrilling seconds of my life.

Finally, he grabbed my ponytail and raised my head up before turning me around and bruising my lips with a rough, beautiful kiss. "You're going to look so beautiful over my knee," he whispered against my lips.

Sometimes you just have to go with your gut, which is what I did. Would I recommend going home with strangers you've promised your ass to? No. But there was something gentle and old-soul about Todd, even as he said those kinky words. Maybe it was because I'd been waiting for what felt like forever to hear those words, to know that it was safe to surrender to them.

We walked back to his place, which looked like your basic bachelor apartment—a giant TV, a couch, a cat, some beers in the fridge. He offered me one, but I just took a water.

"Take off your dress, Amy," he said, watching me. I shifted, not used to undressing right out in the open like that. Usually it was a quick shucking of my clothes in the dark. I did it though, grateful that even though my bra and panties didn't match, they were nice enough—a leopard-print bra and basic black, now soaked, panties. "Now the bra, and then the panties, and look at me while you do it."

I obeyed him, shivering with arousal, letting my heavy breasts fall in front of me and baring the pubic-hair fuzz at my center. He didn't seem in a rush to spank me, even though I was aching for it. Todd walked closer, then hoisted me up in his arms like I barely weighed a thing. No man had ever tried that before. He tossed me over his shoulder and, with my ass in the air, carried me into his bedroom. He lay me down, then rolled me over. "Put your hands over your head. Your safeword will be 'Adele,' but I don't expect you to need it. You're very overdue for a spanking, and any guy who can't see that is a fool."

I shut my eyes and waited, wondering if he'd take his clothes off, too. Instead he sat, spreading me across his lap, just like I'd dreamed about. "Spread those pretty legs for me just a little." His voice seemed to take on a southern twang—maybe that was my imagination, but I liked it. I was already loving this, before he'd even struck me. I smiled to myself—and then the first blow landed. It was hard, and I squirmed, still smiling though. He hit me again, the sound of his hand connecting with my ass loud in the room. He didn't say a word about my size, didn't try to make light of my weight across his lap or the heft of my ass, he just kept spanking me. Maybe he was waiting for a reaction, I wasn't sure, but I could only focus on the feel of his hand, striking me over and over.

Finally I did let out a whimper, and he gripped me tighter with the hand that wasn't spanking me. "That's it, let go for me, Amy." He hit me harder and shifted so his hand struck the backs of my thighs. At one point he dipped his fingers between my legs, and I pressed back toward that pressure, much as I had earlier in the evening. "Oh Amy . . . you need something harder than my hand."

I swallowed hard but didn't look up. I just lay there and waited as he stood, rummaged around, and returned. "Now this is going to be a bit more painful, but you can take it. It's okay if you cry, and you know what to do if you want me to stop."

I bit my lip and raised my ass a little higher in the air, and soon, something strong hit my ass. It felt like a whip, or maybe a belt—whatever it was, it was way harsher than his hand had been. After the first one, I didn't think I could take another—maybe I'd been overambitious for my first spanking. The second one hurt, too, and so did the third. I can't lie: They all hurt, but something happened after those first few. The pain morphed into something else, something closer to what I'd dreamed about. It was like there were three of us in the room: Todd, me, and the belt (I peeked).

He was focused solely on my ass, on making the belt land where he wanted, and I was focused on taking it, on surrendering to the pain, and to him. The blows came further apart, but harder, and I didn't realize I was holding my breath until I let it out in a giant whoosh, which brought on the first tear. Soon, tears were streaming down my face, but it wasn't the same as when I normally cry. It didn't feel so much like crying, sobbing, being in emotional pain, as a release. I was taking the blows and giving back tears, my pussy tightening with each strike.

When Todd told me to turn over, I did so, feeling as if I were watching myself in a movie. "Kiss it," he said, dangling the end of the belt at my lips. I did, shivering all over as my nipples hardened and my pussy clenched even more. "Someday I'm going to use this right here," he said, resting the end of the belt lightly between my legs. I watched as he picked it up again and struck me against my nipples, not as hard as he'd spanked me, but hard enough for me to feel the pain clearly, thoroughly. My nipples, it turned out, were pain sluts, just like me, raising themselves higher after each blow.

My breast lashing didn't last long, but it left beautiful bruises on my pale skin. He knelt on the floor and sucked each nipple until I moaned, combining those frantic sucks with his fingers diving into my pussy. "Give it to me, Amy," he said, as if I hadn't already given him enough.

And I did, though I admit that my orgasm was more for me than for him, or maybe it was for both of us. The lines between his and mine got blurred that night, for the first but certainly not the last time. While he fucked me with his fingers, while he sucked my nipples, while he spanked me with his hand and his belt, Todd's breathing got heavier; his eyes, when I dared to look at them, were layered by lust. Knowing he was getting something equally powerful out of our actions made me warm in a way that was totally different from the visceral heat of his touch. This was a warmth that bloomed somewhere deeper, some place where I'd been waiting to feel adored and pampered. This meeting of souls brought on another kind of tears, ones of kinship.

For all my racy fantasies, I'd never dreamt it could be like this. I'd thought I was a pain slut, a big girl looking to feel, for a moment, smaller, safer, in the hands of a man who was more than willing to give me the pain I craved—and perhaps some I didn't know I craved.

"Oh yeah, Amy, that's right," he said as he bit my nipple, his teeth sinking into my flesh, driving another finger into me. He was grunting now, using all of himself to get me off, and I went with it, fully, completely. I stopped trying to look at him, to second-guess his emotions, to figure it all out. I spread my legs wider, exposing my thighs, my core, my everything. When I came against his hand, the pleasure wove its way from my pussy all the way down my legs, making them tremble, then upward, making me lightheaded. He eased his hand out and then wrapped his arms around me.

I kept on trembling, and another burst of tears rolled through me. I'd thought it was over—that he spanked me, and it was everything I'd wanted it to be and more. But this was like an aftershock, a tinier but no less powerful tremor. "Wow," I said when I finally raised my head from his shoulder. "That was . . ." I couldn't finish the thought.

"I know," he said, gently kissing my forehead. "And there's more where that came from."

We didn't make love until the next morning, and this time, only after I took a spanking bent over his kitchen table, and he'd made me look in the mirror and admire my ass from every angle. "Touch it," he said, and I smiled as the heat there greeted me.

Todd isn't who I thought I wanted to meet. He's not the perfect, sexy, handsome, smart, mindfucking, sadistic dom of my dreams, because I've learned that that man doesn't exist. Oh yes, he's all of those things, but I didn't conjure him up, and he doesn't simply spank me on command. It's a constant give and take, a constant surrendering of what I think I want for what I hope we can achieve together. Todd can see through me like nobody else, can see deep inside to where my deepest fears reside.

Ever since that first night, he's been able to take those fears and twist them into fantasies, to use the fear to guide me into a world I couldn't have even dreamt existed. He doesn't need to spank me to get me there either—sometimes it's a look, a word, a smile, a snap of his fingers. Sometimes I just know. And that's made me walk taller, prouder, armed with the knowledge that even if no one else sees past the girl with the sweet, chubby cheeks and dimples, bright red lipstick, and cat-eye glasses, there's one man who does.

I've learned that submitting isn't about spanking per se, or being ordered around, or even topping or bottoming exactly, but about acknowledging that someone else can know you better than you know yourself, can unwrap the layers you cloak yourself in to strip you down to your barest, rawest, most vulnerable self. It's the same thing good music does, making everything else disappear, then giving you back a better version of you. That's worth waiting for, no matter how long it takes. I get to be a giantess *and* a little girl—sassy and submissive, bold and bent over. And he gets to be all the variations of dominant he can come up with, even when he's sick in bed and I'm cooking him soup. That oldies song, "Big Girls Don't Cry"? It was wrong. Big girls do cry, and beg and bite and scream and cook and strip and fuck and love. We do everything we want to, and sometimes everything you want us to, if you're lucky.

I think we both are.

Marked

BY ISABELLE GRAY

After he courted her for six months—a reasonable time for a couple to get past awkward fumbling, missed opportunities, and incompatible urges—Gideon sent his girlfriend, Felicia, a note.

He crafted this note carefully, selecting a thick, cream-colored cardstock and a fountain pen filled with silver ink. He wrote with purpose and clear intent. As he wrote, at the drafting table in the corner of his bedroom, Gideon allowed himself to enjoy the scratching sound of the pen as it followed the whorls and loops of each letter in each word. When he was done, he held the paper just below his nose and inhaled deeply, smelling nothing, enjoying that nothingness.

He put the note in the mail the next day. He waited.

Felicia received the note two days after it was sent. She read it once, then slid it into her briefcase and left it there for the next week. She had not forgotten about it, nor had she paid it much attention, but at the end of each day—after she came home, slipped out of her shoes, and rubbed her stocking-covered feet against each other—she gave it serious consideration.

Felicia lived a life that was neither average nor exemplary, and the same could be said of her relationship with Gideon. Their time together had been better than adequate, but what she and Gideon had shared thus far was not the most exhilarating relationship of her lifetime. She had not yet swooned.

Gideon was an architect by trade—an artist who obsessed himself with details. As a junior associate in a large firm, he spent most of his time designing parts of a whole—stairwells, bathrooms, windows. The work was more complicated than one might think. His designs had to correspond with several others, all of which had to fit within the overall concept for a given project. After three years, Gideon had begun to treat each part of his life in the same manner, coordinating his relationships and ambitions as individual units that, together, equaled the sum of all parts.

Once ten days had passed—ten days filled with eleven phone calls, three dinner dates, one movie, two hours of television, and six sexual encounters—Felicia finally broached the subject of the note. They were in bed, still sweaty, just after that sixth sexual encounter, her back turned to him as she stared at the blinking green colon on his alarm clock. She slid an arm behind her, resting her fingertips against Gideon's sharp, ever protruding hipbone. She inched closer toward him, considering the contrast between them, the long lean length of him, the soft fullness of her own body.

She said, "Yes."

And as that word fell from her lips, she felt the beginning of something. She felt like she might swoon.

Gideon smiled in the darkness. He remained silent, but his heart pounded; he could practically see it trying to beat itself out of his chest, even in the dark. The next morning, as Felicia brushed her teeth, he handed her a leatherbound portfolio and told her to select the three designs she enjoyed most—the three designs she wouldn't mind marking her body with for the rest of her life, the three designs he could trace with his fingers or tongue or eyes, knowing she would always be his. Felicia dragged her fingertips across the portfolio's cover.

Everyone had recommended Jake, a former football player who found something new to do when his knees gave out. He had a solid name, suitable for a solid-looking man wrapped in muscle and ink. He was tall and bald; brawny and loud. He had big, steady hands, and he always sang as he worked. Though you wouldn't expect it of him, the word "artist" was never used lightly where his tattoo work was concerned.

Felicia sat quietly as the artist held her ample breast in the palm of one hand, his tattoo gun in the other, carefully inking the sharp edges of the first design she chose: three black, thickly curved lines and one red one on the outside that began from the same point, right on top of her right collarbone, rolled to the outer edge of her breast, then back toward the small separation between her breasts, finishing with a flourish along the underside. Her body was, until that moment, unmarked by anything but a birthmark on her left hip, a scar just below her left knee from a bicycle accident when she was a young girl, and a small constellation of freckles in the small of her back.

As he worked, the artist grinned. "You've given me a lot of canvas to work with."

Felicia's face reddened hotly, and she sat stiffly. Jake paused, held his hand up. "I meant that as a compliment. There is no joy at all in inking a woman who is all bone. I like to sink my needles into something that can give way."

She relaxed again, breathed deeply, and closed her eyes. She thought about Jake's words, about bodies giving way. She was lulled by the constant, sharp moan of the tattoo gun and the hum of pain vibrating through her body. As he worked, the artist sang. Sometimes she recognized the song, sometimes she didn't, but the man had a good voice, and he knew how to mark a woman's body. When he finished his work, he stood behind her as she admired his work in a full-length mirror. Jake whistled. She smiled at his reflection.

As she left, Jake said, "I hope you'll be back."

Felicia didn't turn around.

That night, Felicia went to her lover. She went to give her body over to him. When Gideon opened the door, no words were spoken. He stepped to the side, and she ducked under his arm and into the foyer. He took her coat. Her breast throbbed as her body tried to make sense of what had been done. Gideon pushed her to his bedroom, even though his hands did not touch her. The room was dark, cool, the comforter folded in half like he had expected her to show all along. She turned to look at him and quickly undressed, throwing her clothes into a corner of the room. She bared her breast, the border of the new, black edges red, tender. He closed the distance between them and held her breasts in his hands—held them firmly, allowed himself to enjoy the soft heaviness of them, how some of her skin spilled through his fingers. She hissed softly. Gideon lowered his lips to her unmarked breast. She liked how he appreciated the heft of it as he drew his lips back and forth across the smooth expanse of skin.

Gideon paused, and her skin felt colder as he pulled away, lonelier. He nodded to his left, and she understood. Felicia crawled onto the bed and stretched, wanted him to see all of her, touch all of her. She studied his eyes carefully, wanting to see how he would take her in. She saw only desire, as always, and she exhaled slowly. He undressed, too, his body dark and lean, tightly muscled. He stretched alongside her, and when she turned to look at him, their lips met in a soft kiss, and then a less-than-soft kiss. As he breathed into her mouth, she closed her eyes.

Her nipples had always been sensitive. That night, every inch of her body was turned inside out for him. Gideon rolled the nipple of her unmarked breast between his fingers with just enough pressure to make her ache pleasantly. He took her other nipple—the one below the dark curves that ran across her breast and then down the valley between, toward her navel—and suckled it so sweetly, so steadily, lavishing her wetly with his tongue. She arched into him, clasping his neck, wanting him to feed from her. The thought of it was perverse and thrilling. She kept expecting him to pull away, but he never did. He simply continued suckling, sometimes softly, sometimes with a brutal ferocity, sometimes biting her nipple with the sharp edges of his teeth. When she realized she was going to come merely from his perfect ministrations to her nipples, her eyes flew open, and she gasped. She watched the circular motion of his head and luxuriated in his sloppy sounds before closing her eyes again. The way he licked her nipple felt like he was drawing his tongue up and down the damp cleft between her thighs. She groaned as she imagined him tasting her.

Felicia wanted to come, but more than that, she wanted his permission to come, wanted to give not only her body but also her voice to the way he wanted her marked. She wanted to give him that surrender. When she couldn't bear it any longer, she tightened the grip of her hand on the back of his neck.

"May I come?" she asked.

He didn't respond. Instead, he began sucking her nipple harder and harder. Her clit throbbed. Felicia spread her legs widely and longed to touch herself, longed to press down on her slick and swollen nub until she felt bone beneath her fingers.

"Please," she said breathlessly. Gideon stopped, lifted his head and stared at her with such intensity, she wanted to look away but knew she couldn't.

"Please what?" he asked. "To please me, beg."

"Sir," she said. And how the word, that small and simple word, made her whole body feel electric and strange. She wanted to say it over and over again, to give in to the word and to him and to everything it meant when she said it to him—this quiet man who asked her to mark herself for him, who with one simple letter changed everything she knew about him, about herself. "Please, sir, may I come?"

Felicia was not used to asking for permission, not for any-thing. Most people liked that about her—such willingness to live on her own terms, without apology. Now, her entire body hot with desire, her breasts aching sweetly, she wanted nothing more than to ask for permission for everything, to let him control her body and her heart and maybe something more. Gideon ignored her pleas with a particularly vicious bite, sinking his teeth deeply into the soft nipple flesh. Felicia shrieked but arched, offering the whole of her breast to his mouth. Gideon squeezed her marked breast in his hand, harder and harder, the pressure making Felicia's body feel like her flesh was in an unforgiving vice. A curious, not unpleasant pain began to rattle in her rib cage. Gideon squeezed harder still, now flicking his tongue lightly against her nipple. The room was thick with the smell of her desire, his. Her thighs were slicked wet, and the hard length of Gideon's cock pressed insistently against her bare thigh.

"I need you inside me," Felicia said. Again, she was surprised. Suddenly, she wanted to feel his thick cock stretching her and filling her and reaching those parts of herself she wanted to give over to him even more than she wanted release. She grabbed his narrow shoulder, piercing his skin with her fingernails, spreading her legs wider, the heat from her body wrapping them together tightly. Felicia gritted her teeth. "Please. Sir. Let me come. I need it. I need you."

Gideon paused and pulled away. A cool slip of air passed between their bodies, and Felicia shivered. Gideon stared at her body, from her round face to her long neck, her breasts red and hot, the swell of her stomach, and lower, the neatly shaved triangle of her pussy, the lips parted, damp, her thighs thick and strong, her muscular calves curving into her ankles. When he finished enjoying the sight of this woman splayed open next to him, Gideon looked into her eyes. His gaze, the intensity of it, how his green eyes seemed different now that she had marked herself for him—it all made Felicia shiver more, want more, need more. She turned to the side, closed her eyes. Once more, she said, "Please." Gideon lowered his lips once more to her nipple, and just before he wrapped his mouth around her, he said, "Yes." Felicia breathed deeply and held Gideon's mouth against her breast as she imagined his tongue between her thighs, his cock buried inside, his fingers in her mouth, the man beside her touching all of her. She raised her hips as the pleasure finally became unbearable and allowed herself one soft moan as she came.

"I am pleased," Gideon said, lightly slapping her freshly tattooed breast. Then he covered her body with his and sank into her sweaty skin and the wet of her cunt. He said, "Mine."

❧❧❧

The next month, Felicia found herself at Jake's once more, lying on a low, vinyl-covered bench, her back bare. Jake sat next to the bench, one arm resting against the rise of her ass to hold her skin taut as he inked a new design from the middle of her back all the way down to just above her ass. The tattoo was large, spreading all the way across Felicia's back. Along her spine was a series of small circles—purple, red, pink, and stretching in both directions from her spine—marks that looked like bright streaks of paint with uneven edges that reached around her sides toward her navel.

When he first looked at the design, Jake had grunted. "This is ambitious," he said.

Felicia smiled and nodded. "It was designed by an ambitious man."

The artist had muttered to himself as he transferred the design to thermal paper and then to Felicia's skin. "A lucky man," he finally said.

As Jake worked, Felicia tried to ignore the pain that lingered as the hours passed. It was different, the tattoo on her back, the way the needle seemed to dig deeper through thinner skin. The sound of the tattoo gun started to set her on edge. She clenched her fingers into tight fists and hoped the marking would end soon. And yet. She also felt a stirring between her thighs, sharp and gnawing, just below her clit, inside her chest, in her mouth, everywhere. She thought about what Gideon would say when he saw this second marking, this second offering she was making to him from her body.

Her man had changed, Felicia realized, since she marked her breast for him. It was as if the gesture had given him the confidence, the permission he needed (or wanted?) to claim her, to open himself to her, to become the exemplary man she never quite imagined for herself. She was different, too—could feel it in her body, the way she moved, the way she walked around with a little smile on her face all the time. She reveled in wearing revealing shirts that hinted at the mark beneath; enjoyed how people would stare at her cleavage as they tried to make sense of the design covering an intimate part of her body. Men seemed to come out of the woodwork wherever she was—at work, at the bar with her friends, when she was out to dinner with Gideon or waiting in line, holding his hand, to see a movie. The men smiled and looked at her like they couldn't quite make sense of why they couldn't look away, why they didn't want to look away. She was never rude, and when she was with Gideon, he always pulled her closer, held his hand possessively in the small of her back, as they moved in step, nuzzling her neck with his lips, biting her earlobe, whispering about all the things he would do to her body when they were, at last, alone again.

When Jake finished, he set his tattoo gun down. The edges of the design bled lightly, and he dabbed at them with a paper towel. His hand lingered against Felicia's swollen flesh, then slid lower. He dipped his fingers below the gap in the waistband of her jeans, and she tensed, then lay perfectly still. Jake stopped, cleared his throat, covered her tattoo with a clear rip, and rolled away from the bench. As Felicia pulled her shirt on, she didn't bother with modesty. She let Jake admire his work, admire her, and then she paid him.

Once again, she walked away as he called out, "I hope you come back."

When she got to her apartment, Gideon was waiting for her, sitting on the stairs just outside her front door. He stood as she approached.

"I didn't want to wait for you to come over. I couldn't wait."

Felicia arched an eyebrow. Her breath caught in her throat as Gideon jumped to his feet and pushed her against her door, crushing his lips against her. Invisible bruises blossomed as she kissed him back, opened her mouth to him, slipped her tongue into his mouth and tasted the hard edges of his teeth. Her back was tender, and she winced as he pressed her harder into the door. Without pulling away, she reached into her purse and handed him her keys. Gideon opened the door and pushed Felicia into her apartment.

Before she could say a word, he threw her keys to the floor and began undressing her. He pointed to the floor and Felicia fell to her knees. She rubbed her cheek against the wool of his slacks, pressed her lips against the outline of his cock. Gideon knelt down with her and then pushed her onto her stomach. Felicia rested her forehead against her arms.

"This is beautiful work," Gideon said, admiring his design brought to life. "You are a beautiful work."

He kissed along the bright circles marking her spine and then around the rest of the new tattoo. Suddenly, Gideon raised his arm into the air and brought his hand against Felicia's ass. She shrieked, startled, but she did not shrink away. Instead, she raised her ass to him, enjoying the tingling warmth as it slowly crawled away from where Gideon's hand struck her ass.

"Good girl."

Gideon spread his fingers a bit and spanked Felicia again, smiling as her round ass jiggled. He spanked her again, harder, and then pressed down, like he was trying to push through her body. Felicia hissed. He slapped the other cheek, and Felicia clenched her toes. It was hard to know when the next blow would come. Her muscles grew tight, uncomfortable. Again she felt Gideon's hand, and she cringed slightly at the sharp, almost vulgar sound of it striking her body. Her eyes started to water.

"It feels like you're punishing me," Felicia muttered.

Gideon brought his hand—first lightly, then hard enough to leave a bright mark—against the underside of Felicia's ass. "Does it?"

She nodded, her hair falling into her face.

Gideon slapped Felicia's thigh, then gently rubbed his hand across Felicia's ass, squeezing each cheek. Felicia sighed, and just at the moment when there was no more air in her chest, Gideon spanked her again. A hard line of anger caught in Felicia's throat. She heard Gideon shifting, unbuckling his belt, stepping out of his slacks. He knelt behind her, spreading her thighs. He spanked her again, then traced the sensitive edges of her new marking with his fingertips.

"Is your ass mine?" he asked.

Felicia didn't respond. Instead she savored the unexpected taste of the hard anger in her throat.

He began to rain blows over her ass. Before long, a sheen of sweat covered both their bodies. Gideon's breath quickened. Instead of giving her pain a voice, Felicia swallowed it, enjoyed holding it silently.

"You haven't answered my question," Gideon said, lightly slapping the fresh ink.

Felicia clenched her jaw, considered her words carefully. Finally, she said, "All of me is yours."

Gideon spanked her ass one last time, and finally, Felicia allowed herself a long, deep moan.

"I'm not punishing you," he said.

He brushed his lips across Felicia's ass then slowly traced the fading streaks left by his hand with the tip of his tongue. Gideon slid his hands beneath her body, raising her to him, and Felicia surrendered, let her body go slack, let him take her. Slowly, he rocked his hips in short thrusts, only allowing the tip of his cock to penetrate her pussy. The hard anger that had just started to dissipate returned. Felicia curled her fingers into a fist and pounded the floor.

Gideon laughed. "You feel something. Don't you?"

Felicia turned to glare at Gideon over her shoulder. His eyes widened. Her long hair covered half her face, and her brown eyes flashed angrily. Her cheeks were red and damp.

"I feel everything," she said, her voice tight.

Gideon pressed forward, filling her completely, his chest against her back, his sweat mingling with the fresh ink. He wrapped his hand through her hair and pulled her head back until he could see the strain in the muscles of her neck. As he fucked her, steady and hard, he sank his teeth into her neck, and then he said, "I feel everything, too."

Felicia reached back to hold Gideon's body, trying to find traction against his slick skin. The hard anger in her mouth turned into something else. The harder Gideon fucked her, the louder she groaned, her throat loose and open, enjoying the unfamiliar sounds pouring out of her, the unfamiliar sensations filling her body, the familiar but unfamiliar man filling her in every way.

❦

For her final tattoo, Felicia called Jake and asked for an after-hours appointment. She showed up at 10 PM on a Wednesday, just after he finished with his last customer of the day.

Jake looked up as she walked in, the door chiming lightly. "I was wondering when I'd see you again."

"And now you know."

The tattoo artist inhaled deeply. "You smell amazing."

Felicia smiled. "Thank you." She reached into her purse and handed Jake the thick piece of paper with the final design. "This one has two parts." She pointed to her ring finger on her left hand. "The first part goes here."

He nodded. "And the second part?"

Felicia looked at the front door. Jake went and turned the lock, nodding toward the back room. "You won't be disturbed."

She walked back to the room where twice already her body had been marked. Jake followed, an extra bounce in his step. Felicia slowly unzipped her skirt, letting it fall to the floor. Jake coughed as he took in the woman before him, her head held high, her gaze steady. She was naked from the waist down, her cunt shaved bare. Felicia spread her legs slightly and slowly dragged one finger down the center of her body. She stopped just above her pussy and drew her hand over her mound and to the soft skin of her inner left thigh. "I am going to be marked here," she said.

Happy Ending

BY DONNA GEORGE STOREY

Just a glimpse of a glowing neon motel sign along a highway fills me with an uncontrollable urge to have sex with someone I don't know very well.

It's more than just the sex though. It's as if by borrowing a strange bed for the night, I can burrow into the secret depths of another woman's life—one full of glamour and mystery and more than a kiss of danger.

Sex was much on my mind that late Friday evening in May as Josh and I pulled off the interstate into a glittering treasure garden of motels at the gateway to Amish country.

"Which one looks promising to you?" Josh said, giving me a knowing sidelong glance from the driver's seat.

I raised my eyebrows in reply. My longing for a wild romp in a rented bed would soon be satisfied, and I didn't even mind that it would be with a man I knew very intimately already. Josh and I had been together for six months, blissfully engaged for three.

"Keep driving," I said. "You find the real gems farther back off the main road. They have to try harder to bring in the customers."

We hadn't gone a mile down the winding country road when we came upon the most beguiling neon sign I'd ever seen: a blue slipper, blinking on and off against an orange pumpkin. The name, CINDERELLA'S COACH HOUSE, curved above it in white like a wedding arch. Below, a vacancy sign throbbed candy pink into the thickening dusk.

"Oh, look!" I cried out like a child.

"I think I know where we're spending the night," Josh said with a smile.

I did have a moment of doubt as we pulled into the parking lot. Cinderella's Coach House was actually a collection of individual cabins, which, although they looked freshly painted, might not be quite so charming inside. I noted the parking lot was heavy on the Pennsylvania plates. Perhaps the magical sign belied a rundown hostelry catering to local adulterers who were so desperate to go at it that they didn't give a damn about bedbugs and lumpy mattresses left over from the 1970s.

The reception office looked promising though. Prettily framed pictures of Cinderella's adventures from classic children's books adorned the walls. A side table bore a sign reading HOT BEVERAGES AND HOMEMADE MUFFINS AVAILABLE FOR OUR GUESTS FROM 7 TO 10 AM. It took but a few moments for an older gentleman to appear with a welcoming smile. Three rooms were still available, he informed us, but he suspected we might enjoy the Coach House, a favorite of honeymooners, as it came equipped with a deluxe Jacuzzi.

Josh and I exchanged a glance. Hot tub frolics were a special favorite on our sexual menu. Josh loved the way my breasts floated in the water. "Bath toys for big boys," he called them, rolling my pink nipples between his fingers. I always took the opportunity to kneel and suck his long cock while he sat perched on the edge of the tub. For the finish, he'd turn me around and enter me from behind while the water churned around our thighs. The swirling steam, our slippery flesh, the splash of the water as we fucked—it was all so intoxicating, I invariably had one hell of a head-spinning orgasm.

The very thought was making me moist between my legs.

"We'd love to see it," I told the old fellow with my sweetest schoolgirl smile.

The reception clerk introduced himself as Bill and said that his lovely wife, Margaret, had inherited the establishment from her family. "We did a big renovation a few years back with help from the grandkids," he explained as he led us to the top of the courtyard.

Add in the charming little history, and this place was almost too good to be true.

A faintly musty smell greeted us as Bill opened the door to the Coach House, but a flick of a light switch revealed a spacious room and a brass bed topped with a snowy comforter. Our host graciously stepped back to let me through the door first, but I was sold even before I saw the Jacuzzi, ensconced in a lavish bathroom that was obviously a new addition.

"Let me show you how those controls work. It's more fun with lots of bubbles," Bill said, his blue eyes twinkling. The "lesson" involved me bending over the tub while he dictated the purpose of each button. It was all self-explanatory. He was obviously one of those silver-hairs who enjoy flirting to feel young.

"We'll take it," I declared, not even bothering to get an okay from Josh. We couldn't have found a more fitting love nest for a weekend frolic mere miles from Intercourse, Pennsylvania.

I had the first hint my fiancé might not be so thrilled when I started to follow Bill back to the office to fill out the registration form. Josh put a surprisingly firm hand on my arm and said, "I'll take care of it."

"Okay. I'll bring in the overnight bags."

"No, I'll take care of that, too. Stay right here."

Frowning in confusion, I stepped back into the room and closed the door. What was with him? He'd never bossed me around like this before.

A few minutes later Josh returned with our bags—and an even more thunderous expression.

"What's the matter, honey? Was it expensive?"

Josh snorted. "Not really. He claimed he gave us a discount due to the late hour. Not that I trust the sleazy bastard as far as I can throw him."

I let out a nervous laugh. "Wow, what's gotten into you?"

"As if you don't know."

"Actually, I don't."

He threw the old-fashioned key on the bed and began to pace. "You saw the way he was staring at your ass. Taking every opportunity to stand behind you. Undressing you with his watery eyes, licking off the drool from his lips. And *you* . . ."—here Josh shot me an accusing glance—". . . you played right along. As if any idiot doesn't know how to work a Jacuzzi."

My jaw dropped. Josh had joked about being jealous once or twice, but never was it this intense, this real. Still, the irony wasn't lost on me. I'd dreamed of bedding down with a complete stranger tonight. Now it seemed I would be.

"You're not serious," I finally managed to say.

"I am very serious. And while we're on the topic, it doesn't help matters that you wear the tightest jeans on the planet. No wonder the old geezer was slobbering all over you."

It took another moment to catch my breath again. A pumpkin turning into a coach was a far more likely transformation than what had just happened to my mild-mannered Joshua.

"Wait a minute. Let's both take a deep breath. Calm down." My eyes darted to my overnight bag. I imagined scooping it up, driving away from this ridiculous quarrel.

Fortunately, Josh did take a few deep breaths. That seemed to do the trick. He smiled ruefully. "Yeah, sorry. I don't know what got into me."

We fell into a hug.

"That wasn't like you," I whispered into his neck.

"I know. But it is tough to watch other men, uh, appreciating you like that."

"What does it matter what they do? I love only you." I kissed his neck, his ear, his lips.

"You're so beautiful," he whispered.

Those words always made me melt. Because I could tell he really meant it. So what if he was a little jealous now and then? I'd finally found a man who saw my true worth.

His hands crept down to cup my buttocks. He gave them a playful squeeze. "On the other hand," he said, "now that you're engaged, it might be a good idea to dress less provocatively."

I stiffened. "I wear what everyone else wears."

"Yeah, but everyone else doesn't have a blockbuster butt like yours."

His voice was light and teasing, but it still cut deep. I stepped back, out of his embrace. "Listen, I have a lot of baggage around this. My weight. The size of my ass."

"Ellie, I love your body," he protested.

I edged away from him like a wary animal. "My ass is too big. People stare at it when I walk down the street," I challenged.

"I love your big ass." He moved toward me.

I evaded him, gracefully, but it took all I had not to groan out loud. The poor jerk probably meant well, but he just didn't get it. He had absolutely no idea how his words were ripping open old, old wounds. Up until five minutes ago Josh had been the one man who understood my feelings without being told, who knew how to love my body with words and caresses as no one, not even myself, had ever done before. And then suddenly, he proved he was no different from all the rest—embarrassed by my bottom-heavy figure.

What could I do now? Tear off the diamond ring, throw it in his face, and vanish into the night like Cinderella?

Instinctively, I looked up at Josh. He was gazing at me with wounded brown eyes.

The man was completely clueless. He didn't understand at all.

If he doesn't understand, then why don't you explain it to him?

Don't ask me where that voice came from. A fairy god-mother perhaps? Yet it made some sense. If we had any chance of spending the rest of our lives together in harmony, this boy needed more than a few things explained to him about me and my ass.

I straightened my shoulders. I was back in control. This feeling, control, wasn't as old and familiar as the feelings of shame and self-loathing, but I'd worked hard to win it for my own.

"I think we need to talk," I said, meeting his gaze head on.

Josh's eyes flickered. He saw, rightly, that there was hope of reconciliation—the sexual kind. He jerked his head toward the big, fluffy bed. "All right. How about talking while we snuggle naked?"

I almost agreed, but another voice stopped me. *He needs to listen first, just listen, so he truly understands.*

Shaking my head, I pulled the chair away from the writing desk and planted it a good distance from the edge of the bed. "Sit there."

Josh's eyes widened, but he took his designated seat without protest.

I snapped on the bedside lamp and switched off the overhead. The room was bathed in a mellow, golden light. The perfect setting for a tale of long ago. I took my place by the edge of the bed, well out of his reach. "I'm going to tell you a story. And you're going to listen well, because there will be a test at the end. The title of this story is . . ." I hesitated, then said the first thing that popped into my mind. "It's called 'The Story of My Ass.'"

Josh immediately burst into laughter, but I could hardly reprimand him. I had to laugh, too. But I'd have him back where I wanted him soon enough. I turned around and bent over the bed, displaying what every lover I'd ever had acknowledged as a most impressive view.

"Yes, Josh, this is the story of my ass, but it's about you, too. What did you think the first time you saw it? Did you find your eyes drawn to it like a magnet? Did you wonder what it looked like when I took my clothes off? Did you imagine cradling the bare, warm cheeks in your big paws?"

I looked back over my shoulder. Josh's smile had faded. He was staring at my ass as if it were the only thing in the whole wide world.

I twirled around and scooted up onto the mattress, my legs chastely crossed. "I know it's almost impossible to believe a sweet-faced, flat-chested girl would have such a big, bouncy ass, but I bet you were having lots of sexy thoughts about things you wanted to do to it—weren't you, you bad, bad boy?"

Josh flashed me a guilty look and averted his gaze.

"I used to hate my ass."

My tone was suddenly different—lower, huskier. I felt more naked before him than ever before. I swallowed and soldiered on.

"I absolutely hated it. As far back as I can remember, it felt too big. My mother promised I'd balance out when I developed, but my top never grew. My ass just got wider and rounder. When all is said and done, I wear a 34A bra and size 14 jeans. A fairy child on top, an earth mother below. I've learned how to tailor my own clothes at least. And the "big butt" jokes? I've heard them all. 'Hey, Ellie, pull up a chair—or two.' 'If only you could take half of your bottom and put it on top, you'd have the perfect figure.' Ha, ha, ha."

Josh didn't laugh along with me this time.

"The magazines were always full of tips to make myself over. I studied all the eating plans to whittle my hips down, guaranteed to melt the fat only in certain spots. As if. I learned all the right exercises for buns of steel, and I memorized fashion tricks to flatter a pear-shaped figure. But whatever I did, my ass stayed exactly the same, defiant and determined to be herself. Now I realize that she's the true heroine of my tale."

The pun got a gentle smile from Josh, but his eyes were still serious. I could tell he was really listening. Maybe he would pass the test?

"Then, one day, I decided to try something radical. Instead of trying to hide my ass behind skirts and baggy tunics, I decided to accept and even celebrate my natural shape. I'd do my best to eat healthy and be strong, but I was going to love myself for who I am. So I bought tight jeans that hugged my curves and pretty leather belts that rode on my hips and made me feel sexy. I walked down the street like I was proud of my ass, and soon, I was. Because once I stopped hating my ass, I discovered something very interesting. In spite of all those models with flat little bums in the magazines, real men out in the real world couldn't keep their eyes away from my asset. They were positively enchanted. And you know what, Josh? I like it. I like it when their gaze is glued to my skintight jeans. I like it when they look all bashful when I catch them staring. I even like it when an old man at the reception desk in a country motel drools over my curves because it makes him feel young again. Every time I bend over and wiggle my ass at them, it's a victory. And I'm not going to give up that hard-won pleasure ever—for you, or anyone else. I will never be ashamed of my ass again."

I paused and looked straight at Josh. He was taking it all in, lips parted, eyes soft. I realized I was glad I had the courage to say these things.

"But I can assure you of this, my dear," I continued. "Only you will have the privilege of truly knowing my magnificent, womanly ass. Only you can stroke the soft, smooth cheeks, probe the sensitive furrow with your fingertip to make me purr in ecstasy. Only you have earned the right to lick me there—or maybe, someday, to make love to me in that virgin place. But other men—and women—may stare and dream to their hearts' content. Those are our terms. Will you accept them?"

Josh pressed his lips together in a half-smile and nodded. My eyes dropped to his lap. The story of my ass, I was glad to note, had made his cock very hard.

"Good. We're in agreement. So now it's time for the test. Or rather the apology."

Josh leaned forward in the chair. "I am sorry, Ellie. I didn't understand how . . ."

"No, not that kind of apology. I want you to apologize to my ass in a language she can appreciate."

I turned around and swiveled my hips sinuously.

"I think I can do that," Josh replied in a thick voice.

I must give Josh credit for what happened next, because he clearly had been taking careful notes on my story. He walked over and fell to his knees beside me.

Bending close to my ass cheeks, he said in a low, confidential tone, "Thank you for that. Now I'm going to tell you my side of the story."

He put a warm hand on my buttock. I let out a soft sigh.

"The truth is that I've been in awe of you ever since we met. Ellie is so petite and girlish from the front, but the moment I caught sight of you, I was smitten. You're so round and full and, well, blatantly sexual. As if you're advertising, in no uncertain terms, that this sweet woman has a carnal side; that she loves sex and sensual indulgence. Even while I was talking to Ellie, trying to impress her and get her to like me, I was thinking of what I wanted to do to you. To slip those tight jeans off over your flesh; to stroke and pet and jiggle you in my hands." Here Josh began to stroke my cheeks lightly, sending sparks through my flesh with his fingertips. "And I know this is dirty, but I wanted to press my nose against your softness and smell you, too. Sweet skin and earthy, secret, female fragrance. I wanted to lick your fleshy globes all over like an ice-cream cone."

My ass was very much enjoying Josh's story, if the wave of sexual heat flooding my backside was any indication. As for the rest of me, my breasts were tingling, my lips leaked a series of moans, and my pussy was drooling in envy at the mention of all that stroking and petting and licking.

"May I show you all the ways I love and honor you now?" Josh whispered to my ass.

My bottom jerked up and out in invitation.

Josh reached around and unbuckled my belt, pulling it slowly through the loops.

"Now I'm going to undress you and look at you all bare," Josh murmured.

I began to tremble as he unzipped my jeans and eased them down over my hips to my knees. I was so wet, I was sure he could smell my desire.

"Let's get rid of these, too," he said, grabbing my damp bikinis and yanking them down to nest in the jeans. The cool air licked my sweaty flesh.

"There you are, just the way I like you best. The most beautiful, luscious, naked ass in the universe. I'm going to kiss you all over now. To show you I know this pleasure is a privilege you bestow on me."

Josh must have wet his lips, because the first touch on my skin felt like hot liquid. I moaned and pressed my face into the mattress. He did honor me all over, slowly, with open-mouthed, tongue-wet kisses. In the meantime his hand crept between my legs to strum my clit the way only he could do. I crushed the comforter between my fingers, nearly sobbing from the dual stimulation.

My fiancé's breath was ragged now. "And while we're making confessions, it makes me terribly jealous to watch other men stare at you, because I know *exactly* what they're thinking. But it also makes me want to fuck my beloved Ellie in the worst way. I'm dying to do it now. And so I humbly ask permission to fondle you while I fuck Ellie's pussy. And maybe, if you're amenable, I can make love to you on our honeymoon."

I jumped as if I'd been shocked with electricity. Getting fucked in the ass for the first time on my wedding night—oh, lord, the very thought made me incredibly hot.

"Yes, oh, god, fuck my ass on our honeymoon, and fuck my pussy now, please," I babbled.

Josh stood and unzipped. One hand continued to draw soft circles on my buttock while the other pressed his cock head to my swollen, weeping nether lips. He pushed all the way in. We both groaned.

"Touch your clit, Ellie. Touch your own clit so I can stand here and rub your ass while I fuck you. I'm staring at your beautiful ass. It's so big and full and beautiful, just staring at it is going to make me come. I'll bet those men on the street are so turned on, they come in their pants from just staring at your magnificent ass."

I whimpered as my secret muscles spasmed around him. Josh had my number, all right. He knew that nasty image would push me over the edge. Dozens of strangers on the street staring so hungrily, so helpless in their lust for my glorious derriere, their hard-ons would erupt right in their fancy business trousers and spurt a white, gooey mess in their jeans. Even the old grandpa at the front desk was jizzing in his pants at the memory of my ass bent over the hot tub—his first good, hard come in twenty years.

Josh grabbed my hips firmly with both hands and began to thrust in earnest. One, two, three, and I was over the top. I howled my release into the mattress, jamming my ass back against his groin with each contraction. He emptied himself into me with a deep, guttural cry.

The orange glow of the neon pumpkin seeped through the curtains as we snuggled together under the quilt afterward. Cinderella's Coach House had indeed delivered everything I'd fantasized about: an encounter with a passionate stranger, the revelation of a hidden secret self, skull-shatteringly luscious sex. But the best part, I had to admit, as Josh's hands cupped my ass so reverently and lovingly, was the very happy end to it all.

About the Contributors

April Flores (fattyd.com) is a "muse, erotic performer, and model," but that's not even scratching the surface. A fearless BBW (Big Beautiful Woman) adult film star with scarlet hair, Flores is a proponent of the queer community, a feminist, a sex-positive activist, an outspoken advocate of body diversity, a glamorous art model, an avid kink fan, and an all-around powerful woman. She might aptly be called inspirational, fat, fierce, and fabulous. The flame-haired vixen of the new porn order is one of the most striking examples of the new sexy, from her work as a BBW star to her unrepentant feminism and her body-positive smashing of stereotypes. April has graced the covers of *Bizarre* and *AVN* magazines, among others. She has modeled for dozens of fine-art photographers and has been featured in over ten fine-art photography books. She has appeared in countless adult films in every genre of the porn industry (from mainstream to queer to kinky to artsy) and has spoken out about body image through her mere presence and powerful sexuality, as well as through her activism. April lives and creates in Los Angeles with her husband, artist Carlos Batts.

Arlette Brand has been writing erotica for fifteen years, but only for the entertainment of herself and her lovers. This is her first try at publication. She lives in New York City, where she works in a corporate environment that is decidedly unsexy—most of the time.

Tenille Brown is a shoe-shopping, wine-drinking, southern writer whose erotica has been published online and in over thirty print anthologies, including *Fast Girls, Making the Hook-Up, Iridescence, F Is for Fetish,* and *Best Bondage Erotica 2011.* She blogs at thestep pingstone.blogspot.com and tweets @TheRealTenille.

Award winning author Angela Caperton writes eclectic erotica that challenges genre conventions. Her stories have been published by Black Lace and eBury Publishing, Cleis, Circlet, Coming Together, Drollerie, eXtasy, Renaissance, Side Real Press, Xcite, and in the indie magazine *Out of the Gutter.* Visit blog.angelaca-perton.com for a full list of her books and to read her ongoing erotica horror serial, "Woman of His Dreams."

Elizabeth Coldwell lives and writes in London. Her stories have appeared in anthologies published by Cleis Press, Black Lace, Xcite Books, and Total-E-Bound, among many others. She can be found at elizabethcoldwell.wordpress.com, and she happily admits to lik-ing her food—and her big sportsmen.

Justine Elyot started writing for fun in 2006 and had her first story published by Black Lace in 2009. Since then, she has produced two books, numerous novellas, and a ridiculous number of short stories for publishers including Black Lace, Cleis Press, Xcite Books, Total E-Bound, and Noble Romance. Justine loves to communicate with her readers and can be found at justineelyot.com.

Isabelle Gray's work appears in many anthologies, including *Fast Girls*; *Please, Sir*; and *Yes, Ma'am*. She also has many tattoos.

A. M. Hartnett published her first erotic short in 2006. She lives in Atlantic Canada and has set most of her work in this locale. For more information on her publications, visit www.amhartnett.com.

Louise Hooker graduated from the University of North Alabama with a degree in English. Her work has appeared in the University of North Alabama's literary magazine, *Emerald Tales* magazine (volume 2, issue 3), the *Wicked Bag of Horror Tales* anthology, and an anthology entitled *Silver Moon, Bloody Bullets: An Anthology of Werewolf Tails*. When she's not writing, she's . . . well, actually, she's always writing.

In addition to writing, Jessica Lennox enjoys playing poker, discussing psychology and gender theory, and reading books. Jessica's erotic stories can be found in *Spank!*; *Where the Girls Are*; *Urban Lesbian Erotica*; *Hurts So Good: Unrestrained Erotica*; *Rubber Sex*; and *Best Women's Erotica 2008*.

Lolita Lopez writes deliciously naughty romantic and erotic tales for various publishers. When not writing, she's hanging out with her kiddo, loving on her husband, or chasing after their big, blubbering Great Dane, Bosley. You can find Lo's latest news and releases at www.lolitalopez.com.

Sommer Marsden is the author of *Hard Lessons, Learning to Drown, Base Nature,* and *Lucky 13,* among others. Her work has appeared in over a hundred erotica anthologies as well as numerous places online. She is currently working on her second zombie book, and there is a free online novel in progress on her blog, at SommerMarsden.blogspot.com.

Gwen Masters has seen hundreds of her short stories published in print and online, and her erotic novels have been translated into half a dozen languages. When she's not writing smut, she is diving into research on interesting yet obscure topics, hopping a plane every few weeks, and masquerading as a serious news journalist. She splits her time between a home on the Georgia coast and a little place on the outskirts of Philadelphia.

Evan Mora is a feisty femme living in Toronto with the curvy butch girl of her dreams. Her stories of love and lust have appeared in numerous anthologies, including *Best Lesbian Erotica 2009* and *2012;* and *Best Lesbian Romance 2009, 2010,* and *2012; Girl Crush; Girl Fever;* and *The Harder She Comes: Butch Femme Erotica.*

Nina Reyes is a freelance writer who still blushes over the thought of writing erotica, despite the fact that she suspects she will do it for the rest of her life. When she's not delving into human sexuality, she studies dance and art and tries not to kill houseplants.

Donna George Storey is the author of *Amorous Woman*, a steamy novel about an American woman's love affair with Japan. Her short fiction has appeared in numerous journals and anthologies, including *Dirty Girls*, *Penthouse*, and *Best Women's Erotica*. Read more of her work at www.DonnaGeorgeStorey.com.

When Satia Welsh is not completely immersed in the world of erotica, you can find her playing with her two-year-old lab mix or talking with her best friend over the phone. She lives in southern Michigan with the man who is the love of her life.

Salome Wilde and Talon Rihai have cowritten hundreds of thousands of words of pansexual erotica but have only recently begun to publish it. Their erotic teamwork can also be found in Rachel Kramer Bussel's anthology *Anything for You*.

Kristina Wright (kristinawright.com) is an author, college instructor, and editor of the Cleis Press anthologies *Fairy Tale Lust*, *Dream Lover*, *Steamlust*, and *Best Erotic Romance 2012*. Her erotic fiction has appeared in over eighty anthologies. She lives in Virginia with her family and spends a lot of time in coffee shops.

About the Editor

Rachel Kramer Bussel (rachelkramerbussel.com) is a New York–based author, editor, and blogger. She has edited more than thirty books of erotica, including *Dirty Girls: Erotica for Women; Orgasmic; Women in Lust; Fast Girls; Bondage Erotica, 2011* and *2012; Gotta Have It; Obsessed; Women in Lust; Surrender; Orgasmic; Bottoms Up: Spanking Good Stories; Spanked; Naughty Spanking Stories from A to Z, 1* and *2; Smooth; Passion; The Mile High Club; Do Not Disturb; Tasting Him; Tasting Her; Please, Sir; Please, Ma'am; He's on Top; She's on Top; Caught Looking; Hide and Seek; Crossdressing;* and *Rubber Sex*. She is *Best Sex Writing* series editor and winner of six IPPY (Independent Publisher) awards. Her work has been published in more than one hundred anthologies.

Rachel serves as senior editor at *Penthouse Variation*, wrote the popular "Lusty Lady" column for the *Village Voice*, and is a sex columnist for SexisMagazine.com. She has written for *AVN, Bust,*

Cleansheets.com, *Curve*, The Daily Beast, Fresh Yarn, TheFrisky .com, Gothamist, Huffington Post, Jezebel, Mediabistro, *Newsday*, *New York Post*, *Penthouse*, *Playgirl*, *Radar*, *The Root*, *Salon*, *San Francisco Chronicle*, *Time Out New York*, *xoJane* and *Zink*, among others. She has appeared on *The Martha Stewart Show*, *Berman & Berman*, *New York One*, and Showtime's *Family Business*. She hosted the popular In the Flesh erotic reading series (inthefleshreadingseries .com) and speaks at conferences, does readings, and teaches erotic-writing workshops across the country. She blogs at lustylady .blogspot.com and cupcakestakethecake.blogspot.com. Read more about curves and sex at curvygirlsbook.com.